Four Fingers Four-Minute Mysteries

Four Fingers Four-Minute Mysteries

Murder and Mayhem in Key West

Shirrel Rhoades

ABSOLUTELY AMA⚡ING eBOOKS

ABSOLUTELY AMAZING eBOOKS

Published by Whiz Bang LLC, 926 Truman Avenue, Key West, Florida 33040, USA

Four Fingers Four-Minute Mysteries copyright © 2012, 2013 by Gee Whiz Entertainment LLC. Electronic compilation/ paperback edition copyright © 2012, 2013 by Whiz Bang LLC.

For information contact
Publisher@AbsolutelyAmazingEbooks.com

ISBN-13: 978-1493779734
ISBN-10: 1493779737

Four Fingers
Four-Minute
Mysteries

Introduction

Yes, I live in Key West, that spit of land at the far end of the string of islands that stretch from the tip of Florida to within 90 miles of Cuba. Some call it the Conch Republic. Others refer to it as Margaritaville. The early settlers called it *Cayo Hueso,* meaning Island of Bones, a reference to the calcified remains of warring Indian tribes.

There's no point in being PC and calling them Native Americans – for America did not exist at the time. And Columbus actually thought he'd reached India.

These first settlers – long before today's influx of tourists and gays and snowbirds and navy personnel – were mostly pirates and wreckers and seafarers. Houses in the early settlement often had widow's watches on the rooftops, a vantage point for wives to spy whether a ship was coming home or not. The descendants of these rogues and scallywags are now known as Conchs.

Key West is a town that has seen its share or murders and other nefarious crimes.

But it's hard for malefactors to pull off these dirty deeds on an island that's only eight miles square – and everybody knows everybody else's business. Herein are a dozen or so examples to prove the point.

Our deductive sleuth is one Wharton "Four Fingers" Dalessandro, a homicide detective who packed away his NYPD badge and found his way to this southernmost city in the continental US. While he'd rather paint houses and play chess than solve murders, circumstances sometimes require him to call on those old investigative skills.

I invite you to join my friend Four Fingers as he bags the bad guy – or gal – in record time. Sometimes as little as four minutes. In between beers.

\- Shirrel Rhoades
Key West, Florida

1
Four Fingers
And the Floater

Wharton "Four Fingers" Dalessandro slouched in a plastic chair on the Historic Harbor Walk that faced the Key West Bight, just a few yards from Schooner Wharf Bar. The afternoon's entertainer, a popular balladeer named Michael McCloud, could be heard singing about how he'd rather be here just drinking a beer than freezing his ass in the north, a song recognized as the national anthem of the Conch Republic.

WELCOME TO THE CONCH REPUBLIC is emblazoned across the façade of the local airport, ofttimes confusing tourists aiming for Key West. The name's a hangover from the early '80s when the island "seceded from the Union" over a Drug Enforcement Agency embargo, then surrendered and demanded a billion dollars in war reparations. Key West didn't get the money, but it got an alternate name.

Four Fingers Dalessandro was a Fresh Water Conch, meaning he'd been on the island a long time, even if his pedigree didn't go back five generations like a true Conch.

Seventeen years in all. More if you counted in dog years.

No, he didn't miss freezing his ass in New York.

His good friend Dunk Reid was the genuine article, a Conch descended from a long line of salvagers and seafaring scallywags. Dunk's dad once arm-wrestled with Ernest Hemingway. Winner of the match depends on who's telling the story.

As the two men sat there on the boardwalk, playing chess, the temperature hovered at 82°. But summer on the island always seemed hotter due to the high humidity. Four Finger's shirt stuck to his back. Beads of sweat gathered on his forehead, but he was used to it. His cigar-maker's cottage on Olivia didn't even have air conditioning.

Dunk moved his Queen. "Check, you sonuvabitch," he said.

"That's what you think," replied his opponent, taking the Queen with a Knight.

"Shit."

That's the way the game went. They were evenly matched. Their bouts often ending in a stalemate. But it sure beat painting houses, Four Fingers told himself.

"Check."

"Says you."

Four Fingers was first to spot the body, bobbing like a square grouper beneath the dock. A floater.

"Looks like we lost another tourist," he said, nodding toward the blue-green water.

Dunk Reid leaned forward, squinting against the sun. "Damn, there goes our game." He was happy to call it a draw.

The two men met most afternoons to play chess and smoke a Cuban-seed cigar at Schooner Wharf. Sometimes they moved down the boardwalk when the bar got too crowded.

Police Chief Johnny Leigh wasn't going to be happy with another dead tourist. The TDC didn't like those kinds of statistics. Neither did the city commission. "Guess we oughta fish him out," said Four Fingers.

His nickname came from the missing index finger on his right hand, a fishing accident. Never let your line get wrapped around a finger when hooking a giant marlin. Papa Hemingway coulda told him that, he joked when talking about the missing digit.

"Don't think we're s'posed to move the body," grunted Dunk. "Crime scene an' all."

"Gotta make sure he's fully drowned," replied Four Fingers. "Do you know CPR?"

"That some kind of government agency?" asked Dunk, getting down on his belly to reach toward the body. His hand fell short by about six inches.

"We need a grappling hook," observed Four Fingers.

"You try it," said Dunk. "Your arms are longer."

They were. After some struggling the two men dragged the body onto the dock next to a 30-foot yawl named *Euclid's Catoptrics.*

"He's dead," said Dunk after examining the body and pocketing the $244 found in the soggy wallet. He held it up to display the man's driver's license.

Four Fingers squinted to read the laminated card. "Name was Maynard Richard Whittington, says here."

By now a crowd had gathered, emptying Schooner Wharf except for the pretty bartender and Michael McCloud and his backup band on the wooden stage. "Police are on their way," someone informed the gawkers. After that, there were fewer people on the dock.

"This ain't no tourist," decided Dunk. "He's Cuban."

"Not according to that driver's license. Gives his address as Melbourne, Florida."

"Looks Cuban." Lots of Cubans made it ashore in the Keys, trying to take advantage of the "Wet Foot, Dry Foot" immigration policy.

Four Fingers studied the dead man's features. They were definitely Hispanic. But Whittington sounded more like an English surname. His mother used to read him the story of Dick Whittington and His Cat. A British folk tale. "Wonder if this is his boat," he nodded toward *Euclid's Catoptrics.*

"How d'you figure that?"

Four Fingers pointed at the stern. "Says it's out of Melbourne, Florida. Doubt that's a coincidence."

"You think he fell overboard?"

Four Fingers stood up. Pushing his fishing cap back on his head, he revealed his salt-and-pepper hair. Overdue for a trim. "Maybe he fell with a little help. That's a good-sized goose egg on his forehead."

Dunk shrugged. He wore a T-shirt that inappropriately read, IF IT'S TOURIST SEASON, WHY CAN'T WE SHOOT THEM? "Probably hit his head on the dock as he fell."

"Dunno," said Four Fingers. "That bump's got some kinda powder stippled on it. Flecks of white."

"Sand?"

"Looks like flour," he said. But he knew it wasn't.

"Think he got hit with a rolling pin?"

"Let's find out." He stepped over to *Euclid's Catoptrics*. "Anybody aboard?" he called.

"Ain't nobody there," reasoned Dunk. "If somebody was on board, he woulda come topside to see what all this to-do's about."

"Yeah, guess you're right," sighed Four Fingers. His Tommy Bahama shirt was stained with sweat, discoloring the pineapples in the design. His Bermuda shorts were smeared with paint like an artist's pallet. When Wharton Dalessandro felt like working, he painted houses, $30 an hour.

Just then a blonde head of hair appeared from below deck. A pretty woman in her thirties. She wore a red bikini the size of a postage stamp. "Was someone calling me?" she asked, looking puzzled.

"You didn't hear all the commotion over here on the dock?" challenged Four Fingers, a frown on his face.

"I was listening to music on my iPod." She held up the tiny Apple device, ear buds hanging off it like a fishing line. "What's going on?"

"Man drowned," said Dunk. His weathered face matching his friend's frown. "You know anybody named Maynard Richard Whittington?"

"Doc?" Her hand flew to her face as if to hold back the tears. "Oh my God, not Doc."

"Who's Doc?" muttered Dunk.

The blonde started crying, mascara running down her cheeks like liquid spider webs. Her shoulders heaved as she tried to stem the sobs.

Dunk was eyeing the globes of her breasts, jiggling like Jell-O within the tight confines of the bikini cups.

Four Fingers Dalessandro glanced off at the forest of masts in the harbor. The sun was getting low, orange in the sky. "You're saying Maynard Whittington was a doctor?" he continued Dunk's question.

"Yes – Dr. Richard Whittington. He used his middle name," the blonde said, fighting back the tears.

"And you are – ?"

"His wife. Cynthia Whittington. My friends call me Cindy."

"So, uh, Cindy, you didn't know your husband was missing?"

"Like I said, I was listening to music. I thought he'd gone ashore. He said something about going over to Schooner Wharf for a beer."

"D'you mind if I come aboard."

"No, I'd rather you didn't."

Four Fingers shrugged. "The police will. They'll be here in a minute."

"Oh my."

"A problem?"

She looked embarrassed. Not that a woman wearing so little clothing should be embarrassable. "Well, I was enjoying a little nose candy while listening to Jimmy Buffett's *A Pirate Looks at 40* – and I spilled some on the carpet in the cabin. I wouldn't want the police to see that."

"No big deal, this is Key West. I'll help you clean it up before the cops arrive."

"Would you?" She leaned forward, deliberately giving him a better view of her cleavage. It was impressive. 38-C's at least.

"What about your husband?" Dunk interjected. Toeing the dead body on the dock.

"He'll still be dead when we get this cleaned up," she said. Tears gone. The guise of a grieving widow falling aside.

Four Fingers stepped up onto the yawl. Mahogany deck. Polished chrome. Money, it said. He followed the blonde below deck. Her red bikini featured a thong bottom. She may as well have been naked. "Where?" he asked.

"Over here," she said, indicating the gallery at the far end of the cabin. "I don't have a Handy Vac."

The lanky man examined the carpeted floor. White granules covered the nap. Chunks, cubes, piles – like an overturned saltshaker. Bad luck for sure. "Where's the rest?"

"The rest of what?" she dodged the question.

"The coke you're smuggling."

"What makes you think we're smuggling cocaine?" she said warily. "That's quite an accusation."

"How about murderer? That's a pretty big one too."

"What? You think I killed Doc?"

Four Fingers offered her a broad smile, as frightening as a Halloween jack-o-lantern. "Absolutely. Let's see if I've got this right. Your former husband was a doctor, but a scientist, not an MD. He worked at Cape Canaveral on the space program. Optics for the telescopes on the space

7

station. But the president's cutting back on the program an' your hubby was gonna be outta work. So you two decided to make a big score – bricks of cocaine. To supplement the ol' 401k. You see, he had connections with the drug cartels through his family. He may have Anglicized his name when he became a citizen, but he was still a Colombian at heart. Unfortunately, you and Richard – or Ricardo – had a falling out. Probably found out you were having an affair. In the heat of the moment you coldcocked him with a brick of coke and shoved him overboard. If he died from the blow, you'll probably get off on manslaughter or second degree. If he drowned, I'd guess the court will go for first degree because you didn't fish him out."

The blonde looked stricken, blood draining from her face, turning it into a kabuki mask. "How could you know all this?"

He tried to look modest, but failed. "Not hard. The boat's name is *Euclid's Catoptrics,* a reference to the science of reflecting telescopes. And your port of call is Melbourne, next door to Cape Canaveral. So we have a scientist working for NASA. And everybody knows the space program's getting cut back, putting people outta work."

"And the rest?"

"Too much cocaine on the floor, obviously a brick. Bricks are used for smuggling, not recreation. Ol' Richard's goose bump had flecks of cocaine embedded in it, meaning he got creamed with one of them bricks."

"You think you're smart, don't you?"

"Guess I do," he grinned. "Where'd you hide the other bricks?"

"I threw them overboard in a watertight pouch. But I didn't have time to clean up the galley."

"Figured as much. Your hubby hadn't been in the water long. No bloating. Skin tone's good. Water hadn't quite dissolved those flecks of cocaine in the skin."

"So how did you know my husband found out about my boyfriend?"

"Just a guess. You're a beautiful woman. Great body an' you don't mind showing it. Hard to think men wouldn't be swarming around you like flies." He paused. "Only thing I don't know is your stud muffin's name. But that doesn't matter. The police will get him when you tell them who you were delivering the coke to. I figure your boyfriend was the guy on the other end of the transaction."

"There you're wrong. My boyfriend's a lifeguard at Melbourne Beach. He doesn't know diddlysquat about the coke deal."

"Got me there," he admitted.

"Ha," she said, a moment of triumph.

"Got you there, too," a voice said from above. Feet appeared on the mahogany steps and Police Chief Johnny Leigh ducked into the cabin. "I heard it all."

Four Fingers Dalessandro glanced at the policeman without totally taking his eyes off the blonde in the bikini. "So Dunk told you that I'd be in here getting a confession?"

Johnny Leigh nodded. "Once a cop, always a cop," he said. "You're predictable."

"H-he's a cop?" stammered the blonde.

9

"Used to be," said the police chief. "A homicide dick in New York City. One of the best I'm told. Till he gave it all up and moved to Key Weird."

"Crap."

"I keep trying to hire him, but he keeps turning me down."

"Hey, I'm just a humble housepainter," said Four Fingers. He held up his right hand to make the point. "Can't be a cop anymore. Hard to shoot it out with bad guys without a trigger finger."

Police chief Johnny Leigh smiled. He knew Wharton "Four Fingers" Dalessandro was left-handed.

2
Four Fingers
Meets Big Goombay

Wharton "Four Fingers" Dalessandro was nursing a
beer at the Smokin' Tuna, an open-air courtyard
just off Duvall Street. Key West's 300 or so bars come in
all configurations – Sloppy Joe's, where Hemingway hung
out; Hog's Breath, with its foot-stomping music; Irish
Kevin's, with its "fuck you" audience participation; Captain
Tony's, where a man was once hanged; Smallest Bar, with
its four crowded stools; Green Parrot, picked by Playboy
Magazine as one of the Top 10 bars in America; and
Garden of Eden, where clothing's optional; to name a few.

Four Fingers liked the cigar aroma at Smokin' Tuna,
and the fact that it wasn't crowded at 4 o'clock on a
Wednesday afternoon. No cruise ships in port. No
Parrothead festivities or Powerboat races or Gay Pride
parades this week. A tropical storm south of Cuba was
scaring tourists away.

People came to Key West looking for sunshine, even
though the beaches were mostly manmade and the diving
was a damn sight better in the Cayman Islands. When
asked what there was to do in this southernmost outpost,
one hotel concierge succinctly replied: "Drink."

Seems the bar's patrons agreed with that pronouncement. The half-a-dozen customers were onto their third or fourth beer, gin and tonic, or mojito.

Four Fingers had to admit the bar stool was starting to sway.

Just then a fat man in an ice cream suit and white fedora walked into the bar like a 1920s movie star. The only thing missing was a cape or over-the-shoulders top coat. But at 88° it was much too warm for that. Even the suit looked like it'd be way too hot.

The fat man had an entourage: two pretty blondes in low-cut sundresses, and a mahogany-skinned bodyguard. At least the second man's oft-broken nose and bulging muscles gave him the appearance of a paid watchdog.

"Uh-oh," said Dunk Reid, Four Finger's best friend and drinking partner. "You know who that is, don't you?"

"No, and I don't much care," sighed the lanky man as he took another sip of Red Stripe. "I'm not into celebrities."

"That's no movie star," said Dunk. "That's Big Goombay."

"Who?" A closer look revealed that the man in the ice cream suit was a mulatto, or maybe an albino black. His skin nearly matching the white suit.

"A famous rapper. But does Caribbean themes. He's sold a ba-zillion records."

"What's he doing here?"

"Big Goombay was born in Key West. Over in Bahama Village. Name's actually Harold Worthington. His daddy used to run a cockfighting enterprise before the old booger got sent off to prison."

"For cockfighting?"

"True, it's illegal. But he got busted for smuggling. Lot's of folks here done time for that."

"So I hear."

"After LaMont Worthington came home from World War II there weren't no jobs here in the Keys. So he made do. You either played the cocks, shrimped, or became a drug runner."

"And he got caught."

"Somebody ratted on him. The man died in prison."

"Harold seems to have done well for himself," observed Four Fingers as he studied the expensive suit, the gorgeous blondes.

"I'll say," nodded Dunk. "Harold left town right after his daddy went to jail, never came back."

"Till now."

"Till now," Dunk nodded. "Heard he's selling off the house in Bahama Village where he grew up." Being a fifth-generation Conch, the little man knew everybody on the island. His grandfather had been a mayor. His daddy used to drink with Ernest Hemingway.

Four Fingers turned back to his beer. He held it with both hands. Wharton Dalessandro's nickname came from a missing index finger on his right hand. A fishing accident. That's why he gave up the sport. Hooking a giant marlin? Scratch one item off his bucket list.

Ka-Bam!

Four Fingers hit the ground, unmindful of getting sand on his clean Tommy Bahama shirt. As a former New York City cop he knew the sound of gunfire. Sounded like a serious weapon, a .45 maybe.

"What the fuck – ?" sputtered Dunk from the ground beside him. Glasses askew, eyes as large as Spanish doubloons. Obviously frightened. Not many shoot-'em-ups took place in Key West. Knifings and bar fights were more common.

Looking up, Four Fingers spotted the bodyguard holding a pistol in his meaty hand. But it was small revolver, a .22 at best. Not the one he'd heard sounding like a cannon.

Big Goombay was down, blood blossoming like a red rose on his white suit. The blondes were cowering behind a strangler fig in the courtyard. Customers had disappeared, either behind the bar or under tables.

Where was the shooter?

"Keep down," he told Dunk. Then sprinted toward Big Goombay.

The bodyguard swung the pistol in his direction but didn't fire. "Hey you – " the big palooka warned. Obviously a man more comfortable using his fists than a gun. The sissy .22 in his big paw said he wasn't a big-league gunsel.

"Is he dead?" asked Four Fingers.

"Dunno, ain't checked."

"Well, look for a pulse. If there's not one, you're unemployed."

"Damn," the bodyguard muttered, squatting to check on the downed man. Big Goombay formed a lump the size of a beached whale.

"Dunk, go block the entrance," instructed Four Fingers. "Have the bartenders watch the other doors. Nobody leaves till the police gets here."

"I called 'em," affirmed one of the barmen. A bearded man whose bandana and gold earring gave him the appearance of a latter-day pirate.

"He's dead," said the bodyguard. "No more music comin' outta this big jukebox."

Four Fingers locked eyes with him. "Who pulled the trigger?"

"Didn't see. Jus' heard a bang and Harold dropped like a rock."

"What was he doing here at the Smokin' Tuna?"

"Spur of the moment. Harold saw the sign an' said let's go have a rum 'n' Coke."

Four Fingers turned to the blondes. "You two, come over here," he called to them. Trying to sound stern.

The women approached tentatively, not sure the shooting was over. One wore a yellow sundress with a floral design; the other's dress was key lime green. The canary had a baby face, looked to be about 20; the lime slice was several years older, a beauty mole to the right of her ruby-red lips. Both bottle blondes, they could've passed for sisters.

"How d'you know Big Goombay?" Four Fingers addressed the younger of the two. His fishing cap had fallen off when he bailed off the bar stool, leaving his salt-and-pepper hair sticking up like spikes. He tried to smooth it down with his digit-deficient hand.

Baby Face hesitated. "We met him last week at a club in L.A."

"So you've got no idea who'd want to shoot him?"

"I hardly knew the man," she insisted. "He's rich and famous and asked me if I wanted to take a trip to Key West. I thought why not?"

Four Fingers turned to the other woman. "And you?"

The blonde in green shrugged. Her shoulders were as smooth as porcelain. But broad, like a female Olympian's. "I'm his half sister."

"You're a local?"

"Haven't lived here in years." Her eyes flicked around the bar as if looking for someone. Spotted Dunk. "But I guess you could call me a genuine Conch."

Baby Face looked shocked. "You're related to Harold?"

"So what?" retorted the second blonde.

"B-but we did a three-way with him last night," stammered Baby Face.

"We're a close family," the woman replied.

Dunk Reid stepped forward. "Clotilde? Is that you?" He'd known the Worthington family all his life. Harold had been an only child. But after his mother died ol' LaMont had remarried, a white woman. A daughter named Clotilde Ann had come from this late-in-life union.

"Fuck you, Donald Miller Reid," she used his Baptismal name. He'd been given Hemingway's middle name as a tribute. "Your folks treated my family like dirt. My mama cleaned house for them for years."

"An' they appreciated it," he said. "Paid her well, I might add."

Four Fingers was studying the dead man's wound. F'sure a large caliber gun. Big hole, dark gunpowder residue, plenty of blood. "When's the police gonna get here?" he called to the pirate-bartender.

"Any minute. They said the chief was coming too."

Yes, Police Chief Johnny Leigh would show up for a murder. Didn't have many homicides in the Conch Republic – as the Florida Keys were called. The lawman would likely put pedal to the metal, arrive with bubblegum lights flashing.

"That only gives us a few seconds. Ladies, may I see your purses?"

"You think I've got a gun in my handbag?" scoffed Clotilde.

"Why would I think you'd shoot your own brother?" He dumped the contents of her bag onto a table. Wallet. Lipstick. Keys. A book titled *How to Be Your Own Best Friend*. A lapel pin showing an eagle carrying crossed rifles. Chewing gum. A Bic ballpoint sporting the Pier House's logo. A bottle of Evian water. No gun.

"See?"

"Now yours," he turned to Baby Face.

The younger blonde produced a smaller bag. The contents equally innocuous. No gun. "Why are you harassing us?" she whined. "Big Goombay's killer is probably getting away while you're pawing through our lipstick and tampons."

"No lipstick in your bag."

"Uh, I must've dropped it."

"Is that it over there next to Big Goombay?"

"Well, uh – "

He picked it up. "Must be. Color matches your lips."

"Yes, but – "

"That's what we call a clue," he said.

"Ha. You're not even a policeman," accused Clotilde. "You're just a lousy housepainter."

"True. How'd you know that?"

"This is not my first time home. I come back every year to visit my mother."

"She still alive?"

"Just turned ninety-two." Frowning, the woman began stuffing her belongings back into the hungry mouth of her shoulder bag. "You had no right to go through our things," she groused.

"Wanted to make sure you'd dumped the gun, Clotilde. Didn't want you putting a hole in me too."

"W-what are you saying?"

"You heard me. May as well admit you killed your brother."

"Fuck you, housepainter."

Wharton Dalessandro *did* in fact paint houses, a part-time profession following his twenty years as a homicide detective in the Big Bad Apple. He liked the mindless occupation, one that gave him plenty of free time for drinking beer and playing chess and – well – drinking beer.

"Dunk, check behind that big tree where the girls were hiding. You'll probably find a government issue 45-caliber M1911A1. One bullet fired."

"How'd you know that?" exclaimed Clotilde.

Gotcha, he thought.

His friend was poking around in the bushes behind the strangler fig. "Nothing here," Dunk announced, his brow wrinkled in frustration.

Four Fingers sighed. "It's there. Has to be." He could hear a siren. Police Chief Johnny Leigh on the way. He'd have to hurry it up. "Look on the roof of the gift shop," he pointed above Dunk's head.

"Holy Christ, Four Fingers. I'm too old to be climbing on roofs."

"Here, I'll help you," volunteered the oversized bodyguard. Locking his hands together, he provided a step for the little man, boosting him up.

"I'll be damned. Look what I found," called Dunk, holding up a black-metaled semi-automatic pistol.

"She tossed it up there when everybody else was ducking," said Four Fingers.

"You can't prove anything," spat Clotilde. Her eyes looked like an angry cat's, narrowed to slits. Her teeth were bared like fangs, as if ready to attack.

"Sure I can. All you gotta do is add two and two and get four," he said, displaying the remaining fingers of his right hand to show the answer.

"He's bluffing," the blonde Amazon hissed to her baby-faced companion. "Two and two, my ass."

"Oh yeah? Let's see if I've got it right," began Four Fingers. "Your brother Harold ratted on your dad's smuggling activities, got a reward for busting the old man. That grubstake allowed him to get off the Rock. Your dad died in prison and you blame your brother."

"Half-brother."

"He hadn't seen you since you were a kid, so he didn't recognize you when you and Cinderella here picked him up at a bar in Los Angeles. He had no idea he was having sex with his sister, but that's what it took for you to become part of his posse. No other way to get close to him with that bodyguard hanging at his side."

"Just doin' my job," said the gargantuan.

"Wasn't good enough. Clotilde shot him while you stood there holding your dick."

"Hey – "

"Anybody here could have shot him," protested the older blonde, gesturing toward the six patrons who had climbed from under their tables.

"Wait a minute," said an alligator-skinned fisherman. "I didn't shoot nobody."

"Yeah, watch what you're saying," warned a biker in T-shirt that read IF YOU DON'T RIDE A HARLEY YOU CAN KISS MY EXHAUST.

"Ditto," said a gay guy who worked as a drag queen at the 801 Club.

The blonde in the green dress crossed her arms defiantly. "I'm just saying," she stuck to her story.

Four Fingers pushed on. "You're right that it had to be somebody inside this closed courtyard. But nobody knew Big Goombay was coming to the Smokin' Tuna. His muscle here said it was a spur-of-the-moment decision. So it's not likely a shooter was waiting here for him to show up. That leaves the three of you."

"Hey," the thug pulled out his .22 again.

Four Fingers continued, "But it wasn't Tiny – "

"– Maurice."

"Like I was saying, it wasn't Maurice," he corrected his words. "Just look at him. He's unhappy his boss is dead. Or more precisely, he's pissed that he's gonna be out of work. And besides, he carries a sissy gun, not big artillery like that M1911."

"Don't like guns," the bodyguard admitted, putting the pistol away for the second time. "Rather use my fist."

"Judging by that squashed nose, you used to be a boxer."

"Heavyweight. Once went up against Mike Tyson but he knocked me on my ass. A TKO in Round Two. Ended my career."

Four Fingers turned to the younger blonde. "Cinderella here didn't do it. Look at those slender hands. She's too delicate to fire a handgun with a six-pound trigger pull." He turned to the second woman. "That leaves you, Clotilde."

"You bastard – " she growled. Her face no longer pretty.

"There's a stipple of gunpowder on Big Goombay's suit, meaning the shot came from only a few inches away – not from someone on the other side of the bar. The bodyguard was standing beside Big Goombay. But you were directly behind him. He was hit right above the kidney, the same height of a handbag hanging over your shoulder. That's where you carried this clunky pistol, a .45 your dad brought back from World War Two."

"Just how do you know that?"

"You flew to Key West with Big Goombay. But you'd never have made it past TSA with this cannon. That means you had to put your hands on it here. Lots of soldiers brought home German Lugers and Colt M1914's as war souvenirs."

"I wouldn't know how to shoot a gun," she said.

"Not true. That was an NRA lapel pin in your bag. Proves you're into guns."

"If I did it, how come Mandy didn't see me? She was standing right there beside me." A smug look crossed Clotilde's face. An alibi having been identified.

"You're right, she couldn't miss it. And the fact that Mandy isn't saying she saw you do it indicates she's in on the murder with you. She'll go down for the count too."

"Wait a minute," squealed the younger blonde. "I didn't do anything."

"Yes, you did. You distracted the bodyguard. Dropping your lipstick, then bending over to pick it up. A nice view of your bazongas in that low-cut sundress."

"Don't worry, honey," said Clotilde. "He can't prove any of this."

Four Fingers shrugged. "Maybe not, but the cops can. That shot left gunpowder on Big Goombay's suit, so the .45's blowback will have left residue on your handbag too. The police crime lab will be able to identify it, even match up the two residues."

A voice at the entrance said, "That's true. And if we can't, the state boys can." Johnny Leigh had arrived.

"Shit," said Mandy. "They've got us."

"Shut up," said Clotilde.

But Mandy was talking. "She paid me ten grand to distract Maurice and give her an alibi."

"There's more to it," said Dunk Reid. "Harold Worthington was in town to sell the family homeplace, put Clotilde's mother out on the street."

"Also, as Harold's closest relative, Clotilde stood to inherit millions from his record royalties if anything happened to him," Four Fingers added for the police chief's benefit.

"Revenge for dear ol' dad. Prevent mom's eviction. Big inheritance," innumerated Johnny Leigh. "Don't think we have any shortage of motives."

"There's one more," the woman confessed. "I don't like rap music."

3
Four Fingers
And the Day's Catch

There's a T-shirt slogan that says Key West is a quiet little drinking town with a fishing problem. But Wharton "Four Fingers" Dalessandro didn't see any problem as he sipped a Red Stripe beer and dangled his fishing line over the side of Dunk Reid's boat.

"When are we gonna catch anything?" he asked Dunk.

"Patience, jackass."

"Okay, but I think we're gonna be buying our dinner at B.O.'s Fish Wagon."

"I'm telling you there's fish here," insisted the little man, checking his bait.

Four Fingers gripped his fishing rod with both hands, a way of compensating for the missing index finger on his right hand. No more big game fishing for him. Getting his digit caught up in a fishing line with a giant marlin on the other end had cured him of that. Groupers and mahi mahi were his biggest quarry nowadays.

Although Four Fingers had lived here seventeen years, he was still considered a newcomer. But his buddy Dunk was a genuine Conch (as indigenous Key Westers are called). Dunk's great-grandfather had made a fortune salvaging wrecked ships in the 1800s. And his daddy had smoked Cuban cigars with Ernest Hemingway.

Best you could do these days was puff stogies rolled from Cuban-seed tobacco. The 1962 embargo signed by President Kennedy prohibited US residents from legally purchasing Cuban cigars. Not that Four Fingers was enough of an aficionado to tell the difference between a machine-made Dominican Diamond Crown and a hand-rolled Habanos.

Cuba lay 90 miles to the south. Dunk had been there dozens of times, sometimes on the official tour sponsored by the Key West Botanical Gardens. Other times under the cover of night, smuggling canned goods in, people's relatives out. The Conch Republic – as Key West is sometimes known – has a large population of Hispanics. Fact is, this southernmost US town is closer to Havana than to Miami.

Until Henry Flagler built a railway in 1905, and those tracks got converted to the Overseas Highway in 1938, the only way to reach the tip of the Florida Keys was by air or sea.

Back in the '90s Wharton Dalessandro drove down from New York in a rusty Chrysler LeBaron. All ten fingers had come with him. He'd chucked a twenty-year career as a homicide detective for the carefree life of a sometimes housepainter. He was pretty good at it, when he chose to work.

Police Chief Johnny Leigh kept trying to recruit him, but he'd seen enough dead bodies to last him. From time to time, he'd been helpful in solving a crime. But there weren't enough murders in a sleepy little town like Key West to hold his attention.

Besides, he'd rather drink beer, fish, and play chess with his pal Dunk.

The two men had little in common. He painted houses and had a small pension; Dunk was a trust fund baby, living off the spoils of his wrecker forbearers. Wharton Dalessandro had a masters in criminology; Dunk hadn't finished high school.

But it didn't take a diploma to recognize a dead body.

"Fish food on the starboard side," announced Dunk.

Four Fingers saw the floater. Likely a Cuban refugee who didn't make it to shore. They were anchored off Bahia Honda Key. You could see the hump of the old railroad bridge from here. "Better haul him in before we lose him," he said. "I'll call the Coast Guard."

"Better call Johnny Leigh, too," said Dunk as he maneuvered the boat next to the body. "Guy's a little bloated, but I recognize him. Leopold Rivera, head of pipe inspection for the Aqueduct Authority."

"Bit of irony here," noted Four Fingers. "A man responsible for water, drowning."

"Happens. Remember when the chief of the Transit Commission got run over by a bus?"

That led to a moment of contemplation, then they hauled the floater aboard and phoned it in with Dunk's new iPhone. This week the little man had broken his primary rule: No emails and no females. He'd both purchased an email-ready smartphone and started dating Kate Mercurio, owner of the ritzy Poinciana Hotel. "Free drinks at the hotel bar," he'd explained the relationship.

The Coast Guard and police had agreed to meet them at the boat ramp of Bahia Honda State Park. So Dunk headed his boat in that direction. Bahia Honda was out of the Key West police's jurisdiction, but the Monroe county sheriff liked Johnny Leigh and gave him latitude.

The 524-acre state park takes up most of the island. Founded in 1961, it offers a campground, parking for recreational vehicles, rentable cottages, miles of coastline, a decent beach, a boat ramp, and one of the deepest natural channels in the Florida Keys.

Dunk was gunning his Evinrude like a contestant in the Powerboat races. Bow pointed toward the park, the cigar boat sliced through the gap in the rail bridge that had once connected Bahia Honda Key and Spanish Harbor Key.

The sun was in their eyes. Sea spray bit their faces. "So much for our day on the water," Dunk complained over the roar of the motor.

"Oh well, we weren't catching anything," Four Fingers shrugged off the interrupted fishing trip. "That is, if you don't count Leopold Rivera."

"Wonder what brings Leopold to this untimely demise," said Dunk, not really a question. More a statement on the existential nature of life.

"Didn't drown," commented Four Fingers.

"How d'you know that?"

"You didn't pay enough attention to the body when we hauled him in. There's a ligature mark around his neck."

"Ligature? You mean like a rope?"

"Yep, something like that. Look at the broken blood vessels in his eyes. He was strangled."

"I'd rather not look into a dead man's eyes," said Dunk. "Even if he's my sister's former suitor."

"Do tell?"

"That was twenty years ago. Both of 'em married somebody else."

Dunk slowed the boat as they approach the shore. Half a dozen camping trailers and RV's dotted the park grounds, gleaming like silver coins in the sun. Two cop cars were just pulling up, lights flashing like Wurlitzer jukeboxes.

"That was fast. We're at Mile Marker 36." Meaning 36 miles outside of Key West.

"Oh, didn't I mention that I caught Johnny Leigh at a Law Enforcement luncheon in Marathon? He was practically in Bahia Honda."

Behind them, a Coast Guard cruiser's siren wailed like a banshee. Approaching from the south. *Hail, hail, the gang's all here!*

Dunk Reid was maneuvering his boat toward the ramp. "Who'd Leopold wind up marrying?" Four Fingers asked, just to be making conversation.

"Fred Twist's sister."

"Isn't he the guy who's developing that spot down near Geiger Key? Verdant Gardens, I think it's called."

Dunk nodded, making his fishing cap move up and down like a Bobblehead doll. "Used t' be Salty Flats, before the marketing types renamed it."

The bottom of the boat scraped against the cement. Dunk threw a rope to one of the policemen, waited for him to tie it to a mooring post.

Four Fingers wasn't surprised to see Johnny Leigh climb out of the second cop car. Murder was murder. More important than a cop-shop luncheon.

The police chief peered into Dunk's boat. "Uh-huh, that's Leopold Rivera," he confirmed. "Drowned?"

"Strangled."

"No shit?"

Four Fingers pointed to the marks on the neck. "See for yourself."

"Damn, I think you're right," agreed Johnny Leigh. "Leave him on the boat, if you don't mind. Coroner's on the way. So's an ambulance for the body. I'll need to work out jurisdiction with the Coasties. The sheriff's already given me his blessing. He wanted to finish his desert."

The white Coast Guard cruiser pulled in behind Dunk's boat. A machinegun was mounted on its bow. Four or five white-uniformed crewmembers busily secured the boat to a mooring buoy.

"Leopold can't have been dead long," said Johnny Leigh. "I saw him having coffee at Sandy's Café only yesterday morning."

"Anybody notify Leopold's wife?" asked Dunk.

"She's off shopping in Miami. But her brother's on the way here."

"Fred?"

"None other," said Johnny, as if he'd swallowed a bad oyster.

Just then a big blue Caddy skidded into the parking area, stopping behind the two cop cars. A magnetic sign on the Caddy's door panel proclaimed VERDANT GARDENS – AN EXCLUSIVE TROPICAL COMMUNITY AT A REASONABLE PRICE. Fred Twist stepped onto the crushed limestone and surveyed the scene. "Where's my goddamn brother-in-law," he bellowed.

"Over here," beckoned Johnny Leigh. Indicating the pea-green boat. "You sure you want to see him? Dunk's already identified the body."

"Fuck Dunk. Let me see Leopold's mortal remains." Fred Twist was a skinny man, like a Halloween skeleton. But wiry, with the lean muscles of a gymnast or pole-vaulter. Big hands and feet gave him a clownish look.

"So is that him?" the police chief asked, peeling back the tarp he'd placed over the body.

"That's Leopold," nodded Fred Twist. "I'm surprised the sharks and crabs didn't do more damage." Sounding almost disappointed.

"He was floating on the surface," offered Dunk. Still pissed at the developer's rudeness. They had known each other since the third grade at Harris School. Fred was a hothead, always getting into fights.

"Leopold always was full of hot air," the skinny man said.

"Can't argue with that," Dunk admitted.

"He was a selfish sonuvabitch. Wouldn't lift his finger to help anybody, family or not."

"Heard he was a good husband."

"Ruth's better off without him. She'll get his pension."

While the developer was vilifying his sister's dead husband, Johnny Leigh walked over to speak with the Coast Guard. One of the policemen stayed near the body, while the other kept an eye on Dunk and Four Fingers as if they were suspects.

Undeterred, Four Fingers strolled over to the Cadillac to run his hand over the fender. A perfect paintjob other than a few nicks and scrapes. "How much does one of these cost?" he mused.

"More than a housepainter can afford," said Dunk.

That was f'sure. "Did Fred buy it new?"

"Leases it. He's got every nickel tied up in that development."

"You don't think Verdant Garden's gonna be a success?"

Dunk snorted. "He was crazy to buy that dried-up land. Nothing will grow out there. Verdant, my ass."

They ambled over to the shoreline, the policeman following a few steps behind. The salt water was as clear as a looking glass. "We found ol' Leopold floating over that way," Four Fingers pointed with his chin, a habit he'd gotten into after losing the index finger. "Judging by the currents, where would you say the body came from?"

"Somewhere around here," replied Dunk. Meaning the state park.

Four Fingers turned to the policeman. "Maybe you oughta interview the people in these RV's. Ask them if they saw anybody throttling Leopold Rivera around midday yesterday."

"Why yesterday?" asked Dunk.

"Body was bloated when we found it. Been in the water at least 24 hours. Johnny saw him yesterday morning. So that'd put his death around noon."

Dunk surveyed the park's topology. "These RV's parked at the water's edge would've had the best view if somebody dumped the body off the U.S. 1 bridge or the old rail bridge."

"Yeah, check them first," agreed Four Fingers.

"I don't take orders from civilians," frowned the cop.

"Do it," said Johnny Leigh, returning from his powwow with the puddle pirates. "Better get statements before any of these RV's drive off."

"Yeah, sure," said his officer. Not happy with the assignment.

Johnny Leigh turned to the lanky man. "You solved this yet, Four Fingers?"

"I think so. But let's see what your bloodhound turns up."

"Clifford's a good cop. Just doesn't take to bossy outsiders."

"Sorry about that. Would you mind asking Fred Twist to come over here?"

Johnny Leigh rolled his eyes. "See what I mean."

The developer looked wary as he joined them in the middle of the graveled parking lot. "Be quick," he said. "I've gotta call my sister and tell her about Leopold."

"Plenty of time for that," replied Four Fingers. "He'll still be dead when you get around to calling her."

Fred Twist turned to the police chief. "Who's this asshole, Johnny?"

"A consultant," the chief lied.

Four Fingers reached out to shake Twist's hand. The developer automatically responded, found himself gripping the so-called consultant's hand. A little creepy with that missing finger.

"Pleased to meet you. Name's Wharton Dalessandro."

"Fred Twist, but you know that." The developer retrieved his hand, cramming it into his pocket. "Did you have a question for me?"

"Matter of fact, yes. What kinda car did your brother-in-law drive?"

"A Ford pickup. Red with a camper on the back."

Four Fingers looked around the parking lot, then let his gaze drift across the state park. "You mean like that one down near the old bridge?"

"Hey, that's it." The red pickup was parked near the entrance to the abandoned railroad bridge, a massive wooden structure that had been converted into a walking pier for park visitors.

Just then the cop named Clifford Weeks returned, a man wearing a bathrobe in tow. "Got a guy who may have seen something yesterday."

"You are – ?" asked Johnny Leigh.

"Name's Ferguson," said the grizzled man in the bathrobe. His hair stuck up like a mad scientist. "I've got the 20-foot Airstream over there. My wife and I like to spend weekends here during the summer. More breeze than in Homestead."

"What did you see, Mr. Ferguson?"

"Park's pretty empty this time of year. But yesterday I saw a car down by the bridge. Was parked next to that red truck. All of a sudden it took off like a bat outta hell. That's what made me notice it. I said to my wife, that guy oughta get a ticket, the way he's driving?"

"What kind of car."

"Blue."

"Did you get the make or model?"

Ferguson shook his head. "Can't tell one from another. But it was a big car. Long. Like that one over there." He pointed to Twist's blue Caddy.

"Wasn't my car," interjected the developer.

"He didn't say it was," responded Johnny Leigh.

"No, but it was," said Four Fingers.

"What?"

"May as well cuff him," continued Four Fingers. "He killed his brother-in-law."

"Hold on, you can't prove that," growled the skinny man.

"Sure I can," smiled Four Fingers. Enjoying himself. This was more fun than fishing. "You've got a lot of money tied up in developing Verdant Gardens. Everybody knows that. But you picked a bad location, a place called Salty Flats where nothing grows because of the salt. Water rationing's tight because of the draught. But you tried to convince your brother who works for the Aqueduct Authority to divert some water over your way. Guess he didn't agree. You met him here yesterday at noon to try to change his mind. This was a good meeting point, twelve miles south of his field office in Marathon, twenty-five miles north of Verdant Gardens. Things got out of hand and you strangled him with a piece of rope and tossed his body off the old bridge."

"You can't prove that."

"Show the chief your palms. You've got a serious rope burn from when you choked Leopold. Saw it when I got you to shake hands."

Fred Twist shoved his hands deeper into his pockets. "That's blisters from digging holes to plant shrubbery at Verdant Gardens," he said.

"Not likely you're digging holes yourself," countered Four Fingers. "You're the big cheese. You hire laborers to do that. Besides, that salt flat's got so much limestone rock you'd need a backhoe."

"Leopold was my sister's husband. I had no reason to

harm him."

Dunk snorted. "Everybody in the Keys knows you an' Leopold hated each other. That's probably why he refused t' divert any water your way."

"Fuck you, Dunk. You got a trust fund; I don't. Everything I've got's riding on that development."

"You made a bad bet."

"Guess I did."

"One other thing," added Four Fingers. "There's a fresh scrape on your Caddy's fender. Bet if we look down by the old bridge we'll find where your car hit something when you peeled outta there yesterday."

"Yes, but – "

Police Chief Johnny Leigh pulled out his cuffs. "Give it up," he said.

"Damn that Leopold," whined Fred Twist. "If he'd just helped me out, none of this woulda happened. All I wanted was a little water."

"Got any more Red Stripe in the boat's cooler?" Wharton "Four Fingers" Dalessandro asked his friend Dunk. "I'm thirsty."

4

Four Fingers
And the Ghost
Of Cutler Mansion

Mostly it's tourists who patronize Margaritaville, the Key West establishment that serves as Jimmy Buffett's tribute to a lost shaker of salt. Hardcore locals usually hang out at watering holes like the Smokin' Tuna, Bottlecap, or Don's Million Dollar Bar.

Nonetheless, Wharton "Four Fingers" Dalessandro occasionally stopped by Margaritaville for a Cheeseburger in Paradise. He liked the fat burgers, slathered in mayonnaise and topped with a thick slice of onion (if you asked for it). Otherwise, the sliders at Jack Flat's across the street did just fine as a lunch choice.

That particular Friday the Thirteenth, Dunk Reid found Four Fingers at a back table in Margaritaville finishing off a cheeseburger and fries along with a frozen Margarita – the cafe's namesake drink.

"Been looking all over the island for you," grumbled Dunk as he slid into a rickety wooden chair facing his friend.

"I'm not that hard to find," Four Fingers shrugged. Raising his wrist, he checked his trusty Timex. "Exactly two hours from now I'd be at Schooner Wharf for our daily chess game."

The two men spent most afternoons hunched over a checkered chessboard, moving knights and rooks and pawns in thoughtful patterns. They were pretty evenly matched, most games ending in a draw or stalemate.

"Couldn't wait. Barbershop Bobby's been robbed."

Barbershop Bobby was a Key West institution. Not only did he still give a $3 haircut, but also he sang in a quartet known as the Four Cavaliers. Like Dunk, he was a Conch – meaning his family had lived on this rock for five generations or so.

"Barbershop Bob doesn't have any money. Not with what he charges for a haircut."

"That's more like a service charge. To get folks to drop by and talk to him. That shop's been in the Cutler family since Moses was a baby in the bulrushes."

"So what'd the thief steal?"

"Bob's Spanish treasure."

For years there had been stories of Barbershop Bob's so-called treasure. Some said it was a bag of silver coins. Others claimed it was a gold bar. Still others told of a gold necklace – a woman who worked at the Mel Fisher Maritime Museum swore she'd seen it.

"You mean there really was a treasure?"

"I'm sure Bob's told you about it while cutting them shaggy locks of yours. He tells everybody, for God's sake. No wonder it got stolen."

Four Fingers unconsciously ran his fingers – well, four of them – through his salt-and-pepper hair. "Yeah, but I thought it was just a story. Something he made up to entertain his customers."

"Well, you'd be wrong 'cause it's gone."

As a former New York City cop, Wharton Dalessandro wasn't sure how you could prove something was gone that had never been seen (unless you believed that museum employee). But he knew better than to argue with Dunk. A bantam rooster, the little man was tenacious when it came to a debate.

"So why are you looking for me?"

"Thought you might solve the crime," responded Dunk, looking as if the answer had been quite obvious.

"Oh no. I'm not a policeman anymore. That was a lifetime away. I've been here in the Keys painting houses for the past seventeen years. Anything I knew about criminology I left in my desk drawer when I resigned from New York's Finest."

"P'shaw. I've seen you solve murders without looking up from your beer." That was a slight exaggeration, but Four Fingers had delivered a few bad guys into the hands of Police Chief Johnny Leigh over the years. A talent for deduction, like "a latter-day Sherlock Holmes" (as the Key West *Citizen* once described him).

"Okay, I'll go talk with Barbershop Bob. Find out exactly what happened."

"I can tell you that," Dunk exclaimed. "He got up this morning an' the treasure was gone from its hiding place."

Four Fingers chuckled. "Where'd he keep it. Under his mattress?"

"Exactly," said the little man. "What safer place than that?"

"Not safe enough," Four Fingers muttered as he

settled his tab.

The ride to Bone Island Barber & Shine was like participating in a demolition derby with Dunk at the wheel of his pickup. As a genuine Bubba, he knew that traffic laws didn't apply to him. They were merely ordinances for tourists to break, earning the city a steady stream of fines.

Despite its name, Bone Island Barber & Shine had not offered shoe polishing since ol' Coconut Carl died in '92. But Bob Cutler still offered his tonsorial services for the same price he'd charged two decades ago. He didn't like to gouge his customers, he said.

The barbershop was a small concrete structure next to the Cutler Mansion, a three-story Victorian with tall columns, curving verandahs, and a widow's watch on top. The pointed cupola could be seen from ten miles at sea. Bob's family had occupied the house for generations, but now down to just him and his sister, it served as a guesthouse. His sister Eloise managed the famous B&B; he attended to the adjacent barbershop.

Dunk led his friend up the steps of the Cutler Mansion. Located in the heart of the Old Town Historic District, the neighborhood was quiet. Shady trees blocked the relentless rays of the noonday sun. A sign said GUIDED TOURS – DAILY AT 3 P.M. Someone had penciled in the word GHOST between GUIDED and TOURS, for many people considered the old structure to be haunted.

"Dunk. I'm glad you're here," Eloise Cutler greeted the visitors. "And you must be Wharton?"

"You can call me Four Fingers," he said, holding up his right hand to display the remaining digits.

"My, what happened?"

"Fishing accident," he replied vaguely, offering a friendly smile instead of specifics. He was tired of recounting how he'd got a 100 lb. fishing line wrapped around the finger just as a giant marlin struck his hook. A bit of him had fed the fishes somewhere in the Florida Straits.

"Robert is despondent," the sister told them. Even at 80, she was a fine-looking woman, despite the gray hair and deeply etched wrinkles. "I told him not to keep that treasure in the house."

"Maybe we can help," suggested Dunk.

"Go on up to Robert's bedroom. Second door on the right. The police are there with him."

At the top of a grand stairway, hallways marched off to the right and left, doors numbered 201, 202, 203, etc. The guesthouse had only twelve suites, but the numbering made it seem like more. Bob Cutler's bedroom door was ajar, voices spilling into the hallway.

"Jesus, Bob, why would you keep a $3-million gold chain under your pillow?"

"Under my mattress. But I don't see how could someone could steal it out from under me without my waking up."

Four Fingers recognized the stern words of Police Chief Johnny Leigh and the stentorian tone of Barbershop Bob. As he stepped into the bedroom, he encountered those two, plus a police sergeant named Clifford Weeks. Johnny Leigh was a good friend, but he'd always suspected ol' Clifford didn't particularly like him. Probably resented him poking into police business.

"Ah, Don Quixote," the police chief acknowledged his

presence. "And I see you've brought along your sidekick, Sancho Panza."

"Hey, I brought him," said Dunk. "Not the other way round."

"I stand corrected," smiled the lawman.

Four Fingers got straight to the point. He had a chess game to play this afternoon. "Mind if I ask a few questions?"

"No way," retorted Clifford Weeks.

Johnny Leigh put his hand on his officer's shoulder to signal him to back off. "Since you're here, we may as well humor you," he amended the sergeant's pronouncement. "Go ahead."

"Barbershop Bob, where did you get this gold chain?" the visitor asked.

"Handed down from my grandfather. He was a salvager. Recovered goods from downed ships."

"A wrecker then?"

Barbershop Bob held up a hand, like a traffic cop slowing down a speeder. "I ain't saying he never lit a false beacon, but in this family we remember him as a man who rescued passengers from sinking ships."

"You're saying he plundered this gold chain off a wrecked treasure ship?"

"Salvaged it," the white-haired man corrected him.

"And you kept it under this mattress?" He indicated the four-poster across the room. It was a big bed with a thick, king-size mattress. On the nightstand sat a tray with an empty teacup and a plate of crackers. Next to it was a Bible. A porcelain chamber pot was partially visible under the edge of the bed.

"That's what I was just telling Chief Leigh. I slept atop the treasure."

Four Fingers turned to the police chief. "Any signs of a break-in?"

"None. Clifford here checked every door and window. No indication of forcible entry."

The lanky man turned back to Barbershop Bob. "Do you and your sister lock up Cutler Mansion at night?" he asked, already knowing the answer. Nobody left their doors unlocked in a town rife with petty burglary.

"Course we do, Four Fingers," the barber nodded. "Although the guests do have keys to the front door."

"How about your room?"

"Always lock my door. Don't want guests wandering in here by accident."

"How many guests were staying at Cutler Mansion last night?"

"Just three. It's the off season, y'know."

No, not really, thought Four Fingers. But no reason to argue the point. "Could we meet them?"

The barber shrugged. "If Eloise doesn't mind. The guesthouse is her domain."

"I've got them waiting in the parlor downstairs," said Johnny Leigh.

Wharton "Four Fingers" Dalessandro was surprised by the lineup. Not a cat burglar among them, if you went by looks. He didn't try to remember their names, merely assigned colors as a way of keeping them straight in his mind.

Mr. Red was 45-year-old shoe salesman from Akron, Ohio. He'd won a trip to Key West by writing a jingle for a cereal company. *"Tinkles are like moonbeams in a bowl / They taste good either hot or cold / You'll love their sweetness, oh so bold."*

And, yes, Mr. Red was a carrot top.

Miss White was a 17-year-old high school student with severe acne – what cruel classmates might call "pizza face." The girl's skin condition made her extremely shy, refusing to look anyone in the eye as she spoke. Too old for a babysitter, her parents had parked her here at Cutler Mansion while they went on an overnight fishing trip. Chief Johnny Leigh had confirmed by radio that they indeed were on a boat near the Dry Tortugas.

Mr. Blue was an octogenarian who had made a pilgrimage to Key West to visit the gravesite of his brother who died during the '80s AIDS epidemic. Three-fourth of the gays in this southernmost retreat had succumbed to the immune deficiency disease back then. Suffering from severe rheumatism, Mr. Blue had a guest room on the ground floor since he couldn't climb the stairs.

Eloise Cutler stood nearby, as if serving as defense attorney for her guests. Any question that sounded accusatory, she interrupted with a mild rebuke. But as a former New York cop, Dalessandro had a thick skin.

He eliminated Miss White right away. An easily flustered young girl, she wouldn't have a clue about fencing a stolen Spanish artifact. Mr. Blue fell off the list too. Too decrepit to lift the mattress even if he made it up the grand stairway.

And, as it turned out, Mr. Red had an alibi. "I'm embarrassed to admit this, but I wasn't even here last night. I spent last night at the Pier House with a young lady."

Eloise Cutler put her hand to her mouth to hide her disapproval. A remnant of the Old School, she'd never married and was likely still a virgin.

Barbershop Bob let out a whoop. "Good for you, Roger. That cute representative from Tinkle Cereals, no doubt."

"Well, a gentleman does not like to tell … but yes."

The police chief whispered in his sergeant's ear and Clifford Weeks left to check out the alibi. Four Fingers was willing to accept it as true, for there was nothing to be gained by lying about it.

"Johnny, let's allow the guests to get on with their day," said Four Fingers. "They've had enough excitement for now."

The police chief frowned, but nevertheless ushered them out of the parlor.

"Did one of them do it?" whispered Barbershop Bob.

"No," said Four Fingers.

"Then it must've been the ghost."

"In a manner of speaking," nodded Four Fingers. "Your sister Eloise took the gold necklace."

"How dare you," she protested.

"Wharton, be careful who you accuse," cautioned the police chief. "Miss Eloise is a prominent citizen."

"Here's how I see it," Four Fingers Dalessandro continued unabated. "Cutler Mansion was locked up tight last night and there's no sign of a break-in, so it has to be an inside job. The guests aren't likely candidates, so that leaves you and Bob. You have a key to your brother's room. And you served him tea laced with a sleeping pill, so he wouldn't wake up while you rifled under his mattress.

Probably some residue left in that cup by Bob's bedside. And I'd bet if Johnny Leigh checks with your doctor, he'll find that you have a prescription for sedatives. You've needed them to calm your nerves because you've been worried about losing Cutler Mansion. Three guests a night aren't enough to pay the taxes on a castle like this. And Bob doesn't contribute much by giving three-dollar haircuts. So you took the gold chain to sell it."

"How would Eloise know where to sell a historic artifact?" muttered Barbershop Bob. Not sure whether to believe this fantastical story or not.

"Probably asked that lady at Mel Fisher's to help her find a buyer. Knowing it belonged to the Cutler family, the clerk wouldn't think twice about helping her out. But Chief Leigh can check that out."

Eloise Cutler stood as straight as her dowager's hump would allow. "All right, I confess. I took the gold chain. You'll find it in my room. Am I going to go to jail?"

Four Fingers smiled. "Not if Bob remembers he agreed you could sell the chain."

"Oh my, yes. I didn't realize the Mansion was at risk. My sister never tells me anything about the finances."

"I didn't want to worry you, Robert. You're my baby brother."

Dunk Reid slapped the police chief on the shoulder. "Friday the Thirteenth's my lucky day. You owe me twenty bucks. I told you he could solve it in less than an hour."

"Gambling's against the law," winked Johnny Leigh. "But what say I buy you breakfast at Sandy's next week."

"You got a deal," said Dunk, cackling like a demented leprechaun.

Wharton "Four Fingers" Dalessandro turned to his friend. "*Now* can we go play chess?"

5

Four Fingers and the Wayward Thumb

Hanging with the Big Dogs is the motto of Key West's Schooner Wharf Bar. But pooches are not so welcomed as they once were. Litigious patrons and overzealous health inspectors have made it more difficult to have a drink with your faithful dog at your feet – despite Florida's Doggie Dining Law.

No matter, for Wharton "Four Fingers" Dalessandro didn't own a dog. But he liked having them around as he drank a Red Stripe or two. He found something calming about a dog sleeping at his master's feet.

Over at his cigar-maker's cottage on Olivia Street he had a cat. It came with the house. Typical in this southernmost city in the US. Ernie (the cat was named after Ernest Hemingway) was polydactyl. That meant it had six-toes on each foot. *All the better to scratch you with, my dear.*

These many-toed felines were known as Hemingway cats. Truth is, when the great writer lived here he didn't have cats. Instead he owned peacocks, the ornery birds useful in running tourists off his Whitehead Street lawn.

Over on the Schooner Wharf bandstand, Michael McCloud was singing about how when he dies he's coming back as a Schooner Wharf Bar Dog. His little mutt Cinderella was sleeping beside him in an open guitar case. The musician had circumvented the rules by having Cindy declared as a service dog.

Just then, Four Finger's pal Dunk Reid plopped down on the stool next to him. "You buying?" the little man greeted him.

"Hell no."

"Just thought I'd ask." Dunk turned to the pretty bartender, calling out, "Gimme a Sunset Ale, if you will."

"What are you doing here?" asked Four Fingers. "I thought you were off to Idaho."

"My truck threw a rod. Gonna take three days and three grand to fix it." He upended the beer, downing half of it. A big chugalug for such a diminutive guy. Barely 5' 6", he came up to his friend's shoulder. Dunk was a true Conch – descended from the island's early wreckers and scallywags.

Four Fingers said, "Does that mean we play chess tomorrow afternoon?"

"Does a chicken have feathers?"

"Do I take that as a yes ... or a farming tip?"

"My daddy was a shrimper, not a farmer."

"I thought he was a bartender."

"He did that too."

Dunk himself had never held a job, living off a trust fund. Those early wreckers had passed along large fortunes to their descendants. If you checked the little man's Income Tax form, it listed his profession as "bookkeeper." When asked about it, he said, "I keep lots of books. Got bookcases in every room of my house."

An excited voice interrupted their bantering. "Four Finger, better get yo' ass up to Turtle Kraals. The police chief sent me to get you." It was ol' Shaggy, a well-known street person who usually sat in front of Willy T's with a cardboard sign reading DONATE $5 – HELP DEFEAT SOBRIETY.

Four Fingers swung around on his barstool. "How'd you know to find me here?"

"Everybody knows you an' Dunk plays checkers here this time o' day."

"Chess."

"Huh?"

"Never mind," he sighed.

Shaggy looked around in puzzlement. "Say, where's yo' board?"

"Already beat 'im," lied Dunk. Hoping Shaggy would spread the word around town.

Four Fingers gave his pal the Evil Eye. "I'd better go see what Johnny Law wants," he muttered as he paid the bar tab. Dunk's ale included.

Police Chief Johnny Leigh was standing on the pier at Turtle Kraals, watching the big fish swirl just beneath the surface of the water. Feeding time. Grouper and 300-pound tarpon. The tourists loved them.

Kraal is a Dutch African word for corral. This was the site of the historic A. Granday Turtle Cannery, where green turtles were held prior to being exported as canned soup.

"Did you get me up here to buy me a beer?" Four Fingers greeted the police chief.

"That's your usual consulting fee, isn't it?" Johnny Leigh smiled grimly.

"Don't tell me you've got another dead body." He looked around the Kraals but didn't see any sign of a corpse.

"Not exactly."

"What does that mean?"

"Don't have a body. Fish ate him."

Chief Johnny Leigh related a tale that had been passed along by Shaggy's "roommate" Big Dick Billingsley. It wasn't clear how a homeless man had a roommate, but that wasn't the point of the story. Big Dick claimed he'd seen a seen a fisherman chop up a dead body here on the dock in the early hours of the morning and feed the pieces to the fish like chum.

"Is Big Dick a reliable witness?"

"He's been off the sauce for two months now. He used to be a spotter with the Coast Guard, so he's got a pretty keen sense of observation."

"No shit? Big Dick was with the Coasties? I heard he was afraid of water. Doesn't go swimming. Barely bathes."

"His boat went down. He was in the water for two days before he got rescued. Most of the crew drowned."

"Guess that would make me a landlubber too."

The police chief looked at the swarms of tourists in Lands End Village. A huge ship's anchor marking the spot. The Turtles Kraals restaurant squatting on one side, Half Shell Raw Bar on the other. Known by its motto Eat It Raw, the Half Shell's building was once a shrimp packing building. Above it all, the Tower Bar looking like a fire ranger's station. "I've got my forensic guy coming out to test the blood on this processing table to see if any of it's human," said the police chief.

"It is," said Four Fingers.

"How do you know?"

He pointed at the pier beneath their feet. "That's a human thumb I see down there in the crack between the boards."

"Damn," said Johnny Leigh, bending to inspect the severed digit. "Didn't spot it."

"And you a trained criminologist."

Johnny Leigh picked up the finger. "Do you want it? You're one short." A joke.

This was a reference to Four Fingers accident with a 100-pound fishing line, leaving him one finger short on his right hand. Fortunately, he was a leftie. Hardly missed it.

"Who do you think it was?" he asked the lawman. "Did Big Dick recognize the vic?"

"No," he replied, pushing the aviator sunglasses back on his nose. Big Dick said the deed was pretty well completed by the time he came along. Mincemeat."

"Hard to reconstruct the crime without a body. We don't know if he was shot, stabbed or bludgeoned."

"We don't know if it was deliberate or an accident," Johnny Leigh chimed in.

"Oh, it was deliberate," opined Four Fingers. "Chopping up the body and feeding it to the fishes is a sign of a guilty party. That's a tad extreme to cover up an accident."

"Maybe so." The police chief stared at the water. The Bight was smooth this afternoon, as if showing respect for the dead. "Guess we'll have to wait to see who turns up missing. A local, a tourist, a man just passing through."

"You don't pass through Key West," Four Fingers

reminded him. "This is an end-of-the-road town." US 1 ended at Mile Marker 0 in front of the courthouse.

"Well, you know what I mean."

"Wasn't a man either. This is a woman's thumb."

"Why do you say that?"

"There's red polish on the nail."

Johnny Leigh laughed. "C'mon, this is Key West. Lots of guys wear nail polish here." He was referring to the gay population, probably about 15 percent of Old Town's residents.

"Most gay guys don't wear polish. Mainly crossdressers and drag queens."

"True."

Four Fingers studied the severed appendage. "Hmm, that is a pretty hefty thumb," he admitted. "It might be a man's."

"I'll have my guys canvas La Te Da and the 801 Club. See if any drag are queens missing."

"Say, where *is* your backup team?" Four Fingers looked around the square. Not a policeman in sight. "You don't usually handle murders single handed."

"Oh, they'll be along shortly," smiled the police chief. "Until you spotted the thumb, I wasn't really sure there was a murder."

"A missing finger doesn't prove anybody's dead. I'm living proof of that. But it does add credibility to Big Dick Billingsley's story."

"I think you're right that we should concentrate on drag queens," said Johnny Leigh. "But where to start?"

Four Fingers paused to give it some thought. He watched a yellow dog cross the square to pee on the big iron anchor. A woman rode by with a fuzzy white bichon in her bicycle basket. A brown terrier barked from a boat in the Bight. "Come to think of it," he said, "I heard that Bitchin' Betty and her partner were having a big fight at Bourbon Street last night. Some kinda disagreement over their li'l Chihuahua Sprinkles. We could check that out."

"How'd you hear that? You don't travel in those circles."

"One of the guys on the paint crew's a bartender there at night. He was talking while we worked on the Cutler Mansion today. Bob and his sister are sprucing the place up." Having given up his career as a homicide detective, Wharton "Four Fingers" Dalessandro supported himself as a housepainter. "An honest profession," he called it. He'd been soured by the corruption he'd encountered within New York City Police Department.

"Okay, maybe I oughta go talk with Eddy," mused Johnny Leigh. Bitchin' Betty's real name was Eddy Lamont when he wasn't strutting his stuff on the stage at the 801. The acrimonious street name came from his constant complains about how Sushi, the Queen Mother at the 801, managed the "girls." Bitchin' Betty had ambitions of her own.

Betty's partner was a waiter at Square One, a high-strung little guy named Morton Something or Other. At night, he could be found singing karaoke at the 801 while Betty performed in the cabaret upstairs. After hours, they partied at nearby Bourbon Street.

"Hang on a sec," said Four Fingers, pulling out his Nokia cellphone. In this age of smartphones, his ancient Nokia practically qualified for Special Ed. He dialed, muttered into the phone, listened, then hung up. "I just spoke with Michael at Square One. Seems that Morton Canesby didn't show up for work today."

"You think he went swimming with the fishes?"

"That's a question for Bitchin' Betty."

The police chief checked the expensive Mariner chronograph on his wrist. "Nearly five. We might catch Bitchin' Betty at the 801. Sushi holds a planning meeting with the girls on Tuesday afternoons." He pulled out his Apple iPhone and punched in some numbers. "Hello, this is Police Chief Johnny Leigh. Is Bitchin' Betty there? I need to speak with her – now."

The sudden frown signaled a turn in the phone conversation. "Well, thanks," said the chef, then pressed the red END bar. "Eddy didn't show up for work either," he reported.

"Put out an APB on Morton Canesby," said Four Fingers. "He's your murderer. And he's on the run. Also alert the Animal Shelter they'll need to find a foster home for Sprinkles."

"You're saying Morton's not dead?"

"More likely it's Bitchin' Betty who got fed to the fishies. Her nails would've been painted, not Morty's."

"You're sure that thumb belongs to a drag queen."

Wharton "Four Fingers" Dalessandro nodded. "No self-respecting tourist would wear that shade of red. Wanna buy me that beer now?"

56

6

Four Fingers And the Sound of One Hand Clapping

Wharton "Four Fingers" Dalessandro didn't believe in psychics, although he did put store in hunches and gut reactions. Maybe that came from his twenty years as a New York City homicide detective with a high rate of case clearances that some people called supernatural.

But there was nothing supernatural about stringing facts together to come up with a plausible solution. Sherlock Holmes did it in those novels by Arthur Conan Doyle. It came as a surprise when he learned Doyle was a big believer in spiritualists, séances, fairies, and ghosts. Go figure.

Four Fingers didn't believe in any of those things, although there were quite a few fairies here in Key West. Its gay population had done a magnificent job of restoring the rundown houses in the historic Old Town district, one square mile of shady trees, Victorian mansions festooned with gingerbread, stately eyebrow houses, shabby shotgun cottages, and colorful guesthouses proudly displaying rainbow flags.

Four Fingers had been in the southernmost city in the continental US for seventeen years, forsaking a cop's life for that of a work-as-you-please housepainter. He spent most afternoons playing chess with his pal Dunk Reid. Most evenings sipping a beer at such fine Duval Street establishments as Hog's Breath Saloon, Rick's, or the Bull.

Ol' Dunk was a wealth of knowledge about the island's history. Pirates and wreckers, writers and presidents, smugglers and Jimmy Buffett. His daddy had played poker with Harry S. Truman when Harry came down for relaxation at his Little White House – now a landmark in a ritzy development appropriately called Truman Annex.

Born in Key West, Dunk was what's called a Conch. Families that have been on the island for four or five generations. They tolerated the influx of gays, snowbirds, navy personnel, and tourists with the stoicism of a cat in a roomful of mice.

Tourists fueled the economy. Eating in the restaurants, drinking in the bars, sleeping it off in the hotels, buying T-shirts in the shops. They came by cruise ships, airliners, automobiles, and on motorcycle poker runs. Nobody liked to see a tourist get hurt, for that was bad for business. Nonetheless, Key West had its share of motor scooter accidents, diving mishaps, and drunken brawls. But it rarely had any murders.

Four Fingers knew something was up when he got a phone call at the Hog's Breath, a message from Police Chief Johnny Leigh asking him to come over to an address on Whitehead Street. He and Johnny got along well, but it was more a collegial respect between a cop and a former cop than drinking buds.

When he walked out of the bar, he was surprised to see Dunk Reid's battered blue pickup truck waiting for him on Front Street. He would have expected Johnny Leigh to send a patrol car.

"Since when did you become a taxi service?" he asked his friend as he climbed into the cab. The seat was strewn with hamburger wrappers and plastic cups that featured a redheaded girl in pigtails. Dunk was a lifelong bachelor who never cooked from himself. Luckily, he lived down the street from Wendy's.

"Johnny Leigh thought it might be better if you didn't arrive in a cop car. He's trying to keep this quiet till he can make heads or tails of it."

"Of what?"

"You know that psychic reader over on Whitehead and Petronia? Somebody shot him. Guess he didn't see it coming."

The weathered clapboard house across from Bahama Market had been an art gallery, a T-shirt shop, and a teahouse. At the moment it housed a fortuneteller. A neon sign in one window advertised PSYCHIC READINGS. The sign in the other said TAROT CARDS. Over the door it promised Master Ezekiel – Private Divinations.

Four Fingers noticed there was nary a police cruiser in sight. Johnny Leigh certainly was playing this one close to the vest.

Dunk parked his pickup in a space marked RESIDENT and led him to the front door. "You go in. Johnny told me to wait outside. But I know you'll fill me in on all the dirt."

The lanky man pushed the wooden door open and stepped inside. A room that looked like something out of the Arabian Nights greeted him. Red satin drapes and a purple parachute ceiling, tattered Persian rug and a wall chart showing the signs of the Zodiac. A round table displayed a shiny crystal ball. Hokum deluxe.

Four policemen in uniform milled around the table, going over paperwork. Police Chief Johnny Leigh was standing there in Bermuda shorts and a T-shirt that said MY JOB IS SECURE – NOBODY WANTS IT. Obviously pulled in on his day off. "Wharton, come in and shut the door," he called to his visitor.

"What's up?"

"Master Ezekiel took a bullet between the eyes."

"Don't seers claim to have a third eye?"

"Well, Manny Durtwitz has one now," the chief said.

"Who's Manny Durtz?"

"Durtwitz – that's Master Ezekiel's real name. He has a rap sheet longer than his dick. Fraud, check kiting, embezzlement, statutory rape, and bigamy."

Four Fingers shrugged. "And now he's dead. Why the big hush-hush?"

"Seems Master Ezekiel is a special spiritual advisor to the mayor's wife."

"Was."

"What?" Johnny Leigh looked puzzled.

"Was. Past tense. You said he's dead."

"Deader than a two-day-old grouper."

"Any suspects?"

"The Mayor's wife. She was the last one to see him alive. Had an appointment for a reading at 2 p.m."

"Hush-hush, it is."

The police chief led him to a backroom where the body of the late Manny Durtwitz lay on the floor in a puddle of blood. The bullet hole in his forehead was small, probably a .22. No powder burns, not a close-up shot. "I've got Emily Kale in the bedroom."

"The mayor's wife is here?"

"She was standing over the body with a Saturday night special in her hand," said the police chief.

Four Fingers paused. "Did she confess?"

"No, Mrs. Kale said he was dead when she showed up for her appointment. The gun was laying next to him and she picked it up."

"You believe her?"

"Dunno. That's why I called you."

Four Fingers stepped into the bedroom, careful not to open the door wide enough that the mayor's wife would see the body again. "Hello, Mrs. Kale, I'm – "

"—Four Fingers Dalessandro."

He was stopped mid-sentence. "You know me?"

Emily Kale was a fiftyish woman with artificial red hair. Her print dress was spackled with blood. "You painted our house last year," she explained.

"Oh, right."

"What are you doing here? Chief Leigh assured my husband he would keep this quiet."

"Johnny asked me to talk with you. An impartial observer, you might say."

She studied him carefully. "What do you want to ask me?"

"Did you kill Master Ezekiel?"

"Of course not. I told Chief Leigh that." Her eyes were steady, truthful.

He weighed his next question carefully. "How long have you been consulting a psychic – and why?"

Emily Kale nibbled on her lip before answering. Composing her response. "About a year. Master Ezekiel was helping me with some family matters."

Four Fingers let that sink in. "Family matters? Can you be more specific, ma'am."

"I'd rather not."

His voice took on a stern tone. "There's a dead man in the next room, Mrs. Kale. You're about two minutes away from being charged with murder. I'm trying to help you."

She studied her hands. They were shaking. Her nails had shredded the Kleenex that she clutched. "Okay, if you insist. I was asking Master Ezekiel about my daughter's future. Her behavior has been of great concern to Henry and me."

Four Fingers remembered seeing a family photo in the Key West *Citizen* back when Henry Kale was running for reelection. Their daughter was a teenager, still in high school. *Go Conchs!*

"What kind of behavior?" he pressed.

"Boys. Adele is boy crazy."

"You mean sex."

"That – and an obsessive personality. Anger management issues. Sociopathic tendencies. At least that's what the shrink in Miami said. But Master Ezekiel was helping her overcome all that."

"Is that pistol yours?"

"The one that shot Master Ezekiel? Yes, I've had it for years. My husband gave it to me when he first entered the political arena. Right after he heard about the Twinkies man shooting Harvey Milk in San Francisco."

"Where's your daughter now?"

Emily Kale offered a thin smile. "You mean right this minute? She's probably with her father. He went to the high school to pick her up. Those *Citizen* reporters will be all over us when news about Master Ezekiel's death gets out."

Four Fingers looked pained. "Would you excuse me a minute. Gotta go to the restroom. Which way is it?"

"How would I know? One of those doors I'd expect."

He picked a door on the far side of the bedroom, found that it opened onto an alleyway. One of Johnny Leigh's officers was standing there like a Buckingham Guard. "Oops," he said, then tried the door to the right. The dingy bathroom he encountered smelled of chlorine and toothpaste.

First, he checked the medicine cabinet, inventorying its contents. Bayer aspirin, vitamin B-12, Pepto-Bismol, a bottle of purple pills, shaving cream, and a Mennen Speed Stick. No condoms. So much for that.

Pulling out his cheap Nokia cellphone, he dialed two numbers, flushed the commode to make his absence sound authentic, then stepped back into the bedroom.

He walked to the nightstand and checked the drawer. A cheap paperback titled *Teenage Sex Slave*, a bill from Keys Energy, a red-and-white pack of Marlboros, and some Tic Tacs. No condoms.

Emily Kale interrupted his rummaging. "Do you have any more questions for me?" Her hands were still shaking. A mild form of palsy, he figured.

"No ma'am. I think we're ready to talk to the chief." He tapped on the door and Johnny Leigh slipped into the room, carefully blocking her view of the dead body.

"You figured it out yet?" the chief asked him.

"Just one more thing. Could I see the swami's appointment book?"

"Got it right here." The lawmen handed over a dime-store composition notebook.

Four Fingers flipped the pages, using the index finger of his left hand. The only one he had, following that stupid fishing accident a few years ago. "Here we go," he said, coming to today's date. "2:00 Kale, it says."

Chief Leigh nodded. "See, I told you Emily was the last to see Manny Durtwitz alive."

"Wrong, it was Adele Kale, not Emily. She's covering for her daughter."

"No, no," the mayor's wife screamed. "That's a lie."

Four Fingers Dalessandro shook his head, ruffling his salt-and-pepper hair with the effort. "Sorry, ma'am, but here's what happened. You've been sending your daughter to see Master Ezekiel. He's been counseling her for sex addiction. But Manny Durtwitz – that was his real name – was a con man who took advantage of your daughter. The book in his nightstand proves he had a thing for young girls. And the Viagra in his medicine cabinet says he was sexually active. But the lack of condoms indicates he was reckless. Adele turned up pregnant. Her homeroom teacher who I talked with a few minutes ago says your

64

daughter's been sick lately. Durtwitz had no intention of marrying her. He's a convicted bigamist, already got two wives. Didn't need another bride. Having anger issues, Adele brought your gun with her to today's session and shot him. No, she wasn't at school today, according to her teacher."

"Son of a gun," said Johnny Leigh.

"You've got it wrong," cried Emily Kale. "I shot him for what he did to Adele."

"No, ma'am. You noticed the gun missing and came here to head off Adele. But you arrived too late. So you called your husband to pick her up and leave you to take the blame. I just spoke to his secretary who confirmed that you left a message for Mayor Kale to pick up his daughter at this street address. Since the police have kept the lid on this, his secretary had no idea anything was wrong and was quite chatty. She's my friend Dunk's cousin, met me at a party. I can be charming."

"You can't prove any of this," shouted the mayor's wife.

"A pregnancy test will confirm Adele's condition. And there's probably gunpowder residue on her hands. Besides, with your shaky hands you never could have made that shot. Adele was standing a good ten feet away when she popped him. Not bad shooting with a handgun. Right between the eyes."

"Oh dear," the woman sobbed. "What will happen to my daughter?"

Four Fingers glanced at Johnny Leigh for confirmation. "Not much. She's underage, the victim of statutory rape. Plus she shot Master Ezekiel in self-defense."

"H-how do you know that?"

"I don't. But the chief might just find a pistol that belongs to Manny Durtwitz if he looks hard enough. That would be a decent outcome."

"Yes," nodded the police chief. "I promise to search till I find that gun. There are plenty of unregistered firearms floating around town. One might turn up here."

"My husband will be most grateful," said Emily Kale. "To both of you."

"Then," said Wharton "Four Fingers" Dalessandro, "do you think he could pay me the balance he still owes for my painting your house?"

7

Four Fingers
And the Poinciana
Safe Crackers

Wharton "Four Fingers" Dalessandro wasn't one for high teas and finger sandwich (no pun intended), but he wound up at a fancy Sunday afternoon gathering at the Poinciana Hotel a few weeks ago. Seems his pal Dunk Reid was dating the hotel owner, a fiery redhead known as Kiss Me Kate. At least that's what Katherine Mercurio's friends called her behind her back.

Kate was what you might call a Merry Widow. She'd inherited the upscale garden hotel from her late husband, a still-in-the-closet gay who liked having a wife as his beard. Trouble was, ol' Carl Mercurio and his wife were attracted to the same type of men – dark Latino Lotharios.

But lately she'd being seeing Dunk, who was neither dark nor Latino. A fifth generation Conch, he was descended from British pirates and wreckers. Those rogues who'd settled Key West in the late 1700s.

Named Cayo Hueso by the Spanish, the early mapmakers had phonetically transferred it as Key West. Nothing to do with the island's westerly location at the tip end of the Florida Keys. In fact, the name literally means "island of bones," a reference to the remains of warring Indian tribes found by Spanish explorers.

Although not Kate's usual type, Dunk did have something going for him: a large trust fund. Those wrecker forbearers had hauled in enough gold and silver from downed Spanish treasure ships to take care of the family for generations to come.

Kate Mercurio was swirling about the Poinciana's garden, greeting guests and locales while a string quartet played a ditty by Wolfgang Mozart. What Dunk called "chamber-pot music."

The cultural divide between the little man and his current paramour seem to make little difference. She showed him off like a trophy catch from a deep-sea fishing expedition. The island was overrun by bachelors on the prowl, but eligible bachelors (i.e. single heterosexual guys with money) were hard to come by.

At 5' 6", Dunk's shock of gray hair barely came up to Kate's shoulder. Her skin was fair, but freckled, a sharp contrast to Dunk's sea-weathered face. Her thick red lipstick matched the artificial color of her wavy hair. So did her cocktail dress, a $600 original designed by Sushi (a local drag queen and expert seamstress).

Being straight, Dunk had never been in the 801 Club's upstairs cabaret where Sushi and the "girls" performed. Kate sometimes went there with her friends on Sunday afternoons for Gay Bingo. A drag queen drawing numbers with lots of audience participation. Kate sat at a table where the non-gay patrons wore T-shirts that said DO NOT FEED OR TEASE THE STRAIGHT PEOPLE.

All in good fun.

This particular Sunday afternoon, Four Fingers Dalessandro was wearing a cream-colored tropical suit, a far cry from his usual rags as a housepainter. He'd given up a twenty-year career as a New York City homicide detective to come to this southernmost city to do the mindless occupation of painting houses.

Since there were only 3,000 houses in the Old Town section of Key West, and the Historical Architect Review Commission maintained strict guidelines as to allowable exterior colors, Four Fingers didn't have to give much thought to the Benjamin Moore paints he got at Strunk's Ace Hardware.

His mental exercise came from games of chess with Dunk, a daily occurrence at Schooner Wharf Bar. He'd rather be defending his King's position than drinking tea from dainty china cups here at the Poinciana. But he'd promised Dunk to be supportive of this new relationship. He hoped the little man wasn't wearing his heart on his sleeve, for everyone knew Kiss Me Kate was a man-eater.

Just then Kate Mercurio appeared at Four Finger's side and whispered in his ear, "Can I see you in private, Wharton?"

Uh-oh. Privacy with Kate was like stepping alone into a tiger pit at the zoo. "Sure," he said politely, all the while casting his eyes about the garden for his pal Dunk. Like looking for a lifeline for a sinking ship.

They stepped into a side parlor of the Poinciana, a room dominated by a stylish grand piano. Steinway stamped on the polish wood. A chandelier hanged from the ceiling. Numerous paintings (well, reproductions) of Audubon birds made the room seem like an aviary.

"I've just been robbed," she said.

The words caught Four Fingers by surprise. "You mean a stickup? Or a burglary?"

"Someone cracked my safe while we were watching Mayor Kale draw this week's lottery winner." While not technically a lottery, each week a lucky guest won a dinner-for-two at Red Kate's, the hotel's four-star seafood restaurant. Kate's brother Jon was a Le Cordon Blue-trained chef. His twin Don ran a fishing boat.

"How much money's missing?"

"Ten thousand dollars, give or take. I forgot to make this week's bank deposit."

"Who knew you had that much money in the same?"

"Nobody. Except my staff."

"Did the thief blow the safe? I didn't hear any explosion. And that Mozart music's not very loud."

"No, the door was standing open."

She led him to her small office, to the right of the stairwell off the lobby. "See?" she pointed. The room was neat as a pin, not a paper out of place. The door to the four-foot-tall metal safe stood open like an invitation to look inside. He did, noting an open moneybox. It was empty.

"An inside job," Four Finger's concluded. "This is an Ilco 673, a high security safe that's pretty much pick-proof and drill-proof. It was opened by somebody who already had the combination."

"Nobody has the combination but me. And my brothers."

"Are they here?"

"Yes, but surely you don't suspect Jon or Don."

"Maybe they gave the combination to someone they trusted," he said, not believing that theory for a second.

Turns out, Jon and Don were redheads just like sister Kate. They were as interchangeable as Ken Dolls. Other than that they shared a tuxedo. Jon (or was it Don?) wore a tux jacket and Bermuda shorts; Don (or was it Jon?) wore tuxedo trousers but a T-shirt that said PRESERVE THE WHALES – THEY'RE DELICIOUS AS LEFTOVERS. Key West formal.

"You must be the chef," Four Fingers said to the guy in the T-shirt.

"Nope, the fisherman."

"Sorry. Need to ask you guys a couple of questions."

"Sure, whatzup?" said Don.

"Ditto," said Jon.

"You guys know the combination to the hotel safe? Does anyone else? A girlfriend? A hotel employee?"

"Nobody but us," answered Jon.

"Just us," agreed Don.

"Have either of you opened the safe today?"

The chef shook his head. So did the boat captain.

"Somebody opened it and nabbed a big chunk of change," Four Fingers told them. "So think hard about who else might've known that combination. Otherwise the police are gonna be focusing on you three."

"Me too?" squealed Kate. "But I'm the one who reported it to you."

"Police Chief Johnny Leigh will say if you three are the only ones who knew the combination, then one of you had to be the guilty party."

The door opened and Dunk Reid stuck his head in. His

hair was as unruly as usual, but he had a cockeyed grin on his face that said he'd been drinking more than Camembert tea. "There you are, hon," he said to Kate. "Been looking all over for you." Noticing the presence of Four Fingers and the two brothers, his forehead wrinkled with puzzlement. "Hey, what's going on?" he inquired.

"Somebody robbed the safe," wailed Kate. "The thief took all the money. Nearly ten thousand dollars – gone!"

"Gee, hon, that's terrible," said Dunk. "Ten grand, that's nearly what you owe the tax guys."

"Dunk sweetie, no need to discuss my personal finances with my brothers and your friend. Let's concentrate on finding the culprit who robbed the safe."

"That's easy," said Four Fingers. "Her brother Don did it. Stole the money to pay off the mortgage on his boat."

"Hey – " protested the guy in the T-shirt. "That's not true."

"Don doesn't owe any money on his boat," his brother came to his defense. "We're partners in it. Bought it free and clear."

"Then you're in it together. Kate, you can call the police now. Johnny Leigh will come down and take them both into custody."

"No, not my brothers."

"They robbed you."

"No, they didn't. I took the money myself to pay off that tax lien. "But I didn't want Jon and Don to know about it. They're partners in the hotel too."

"Katie, you were trying to cheat us?" said Jon, shocked by his sister's confession.

"Your own brothers," added Don. "Mom would be

ashamed of you."

Kate Mercurio stamped her foot. "You weren't going to lose a dime. The hotel's insurance would have covered it."

"That might be considered a crime in some circles," allowed Four Fingers. His impulse was to point a finger of guilt at her, put his missing index finger made that difficult.

"Hon, you didn't have to take the hotel's money," said Dunk as he stepped into the room. "I was going to put up the ten grand for you."

"Thank you, sweetie. But now it's too late."

"Not at all," argued Dunk. "You can put the money back in the safe. I'll write a check to the IRS tomorrow. And we can forget about this."

"Great idea," said Jon.

"Ditto," said Don.

"Could we do that, Wharton?" Kate Mercurio batted her lashes at him.

"If it's okay with Dunk, it's okay with me."

"Thank you. I'm glad we didn't have to bring the police into this."

"Oh, we might yet."

Kiss Me Kate paused. "Whatever do you mean?"

Four Fingers turned to his friend. "Dunk, what made you come looking for Kate just now?"

The little man looked flustered. "Well, uh, a waiter delivered this note." He handed it over.

> *Kate wants you to meet her in the*
> *office right away.*
>
> > *Jon*

"There you have it," said Four Fingers. This note was designed to get you in here just as I figured out Kate took the money so you could play White Knight and save her. The fact that her brother Jon sent the note proves all three were in on the scam. The twin brothers were partners in everything – boat hotel, I even heard they were both dating the same woman."

"Mary Beth Higginsby? Yeah, I heard the same thing," nodded Dunk, still looking discombobulated. "Her husband left her for one of the Czech strippers at Bare Assets about six months ago."

"Dunk sweetie, you can't believe that my brothers and I were trying to con you out of ten thousand dollars," wheedled Kate, offering him a plaintive look like one of those old Kean paintings. "You're my little conch fritter."

Dunk Reid shrugged resignedly. "Never did understand what Kiss Me Kate saw in me," he said to Four Fingers. "I sure ain't the tall, dark Latin type. But I do have a lotto money."

"Wanna go up to Schooner Wharf and have a beer?"

"Why not? I don't even like tea."

"What about the police?" asked Kate Mercurio, glancing nervously at her two brothers, then at Four Fingers.

"Up to your boyfriend."

"Former boyfriend," said Dunk. "I'm going back to my policy of no emails and no females. But I don't see no reason t' tell Johnny Leigh about this. Turns out, nothing got stolen ... from anybody."

"Can we order a couple of juicy hamburgers to go with

the beer?" said Wharton "Four Fingers" Dalessandro. "Those li'l cucumber sandwiches just aren't filling."

8

Four Fingers
And the Full Hand

Wharton "Four Fingers" Dalessandro wasn't much of a gambler, although he did play chess with his friend Dunk Reid for $10 a game. Although they played daily at Schooner Wharf Bar, the balance sheet was pretty even because the men were well matched – more stalemates than outright wins.

He heard about the poker game from Richard Starkwell, one of the partners of Starkwell and Starkwell, the preeminent law firm in Key West. The Starkwell brothers owned a big chunk of the island, having the inside track on most of the deals that pass through the county courthouse. The Starkwells were an old Conch family, their antecedents being five generations of pirates and smugglers and salvagers.

Things hadn't changed much.

Back when President Harry S. Truman relaxed at the Little White House, he used to play poker with local pals. Those were the days when a president could walk down Duval Street without a contingent of Secret Service bodyguards surrounding him.

When Captain Tony – namesake of the famous bar – landed in Key West, the town was rife with prostitution and gambling. "I'm home," he declared.

Key West is not so much a gambling destination these days, although there's a strong movement to legalize casino gambling, more as a lure for tourists than a quest for riches. Or are those the same thing?

The only reason Four Fingers Dalessandro got invited to the poker game was because he'd been painting Richard's house that day and the boys came up one short for their usual Wednesday night poker game. Everybody knew Four Fingers used to be a homicide cop in New York City before packing it in and moving to the southernmost point in the continental US. So he got some residual respect, even though he made his living as a lowly housepainter.

That and the fact he was best friends with Dunk Reid, one of the richest Conchs on the island. Not that you'd ever know it by the battered truck Dunk drove or the rumpled clothes he wore.

"Can you afford it?" asked Richard Starkwell. "The pots get kinda pricey."

"I can hold my own," shrugged Four Fingers. "I bank most of my house painting money; live off my police pension."

"Well, if you're sure. Mayor Kale didn't drop out till half hour ago, so I appreciate your filling his spot."

The weekly games took place in a suite at the Bight Hotel. The Starkwells owned it through a series of holding corporations. The suite's living room featured a well-stocked bar and a round table with seven chairs. One door led to a bedroom, the other to a large bath. The walls were decorated with original Mario Sanchez wood paintings – colorful scenes of Old Key West.

"We've got a guest sitting in for Henry Kale tonight," Richard presented Wharton Dalessandro. The players included Daniel Wallowicz, a large landholder; Tobias Newcastle, a city commissioner; Rev. Benjamin Willingham, pastor of the Fisher of Men Church; and Judge J. Randall Barbareau. The seventh man – Richard's brother Thomas – was in the bedroom changing into casual clothing after a day in court.

"Thanks for letting me join you," said Four Fingers. "I didn't expect to be in such exalted company."

"Dunk speaks highly of you," smiled Daniel Wallowicz. The old slumlord must have been 90 years old, judging by his mummified skin.

"So does the police chief," nodded Judge Barbareau. He was a distinguished-looking gentleman with a potbelly and slicked-back silver hair. "Says you've helped him solve a few murders."

"Once a homicide cop, always a homicide cop," commented the city commissioner. He oversaw the Police Review Board, among other duties.

"I sure hope not," sighed Four Fingers. "I'm just trying to be a house painter."

"And he's doing a fine job on my place," said Richard Starkwell. He and his wife Betsy had a classic temple revival style house on Williams Street. Quite a showplace, it had been on the annual House Tour three times.

"Thomas won the pot last week," Daniel Wallowicz turned the conversation back to the game: Texas Holdem. "Took us for ten grand each."

Holy crap, thought Four Fingers Dalessandro. *I'm in over my head.* But he merely shrugged and said, "I hope you boys accept IOU's."

The men chuckled as if he'd just told a good joke about a rabbi, a monkey, and a chicken walking into a bar.

"Where *is* ol' Tommy Boy?" asked Richard, looking around the room.

"Changing clothes in the bedroom. You'd better go get him or he'll be in there all night," said Toby Newcastle.

"Yes, your brother does exhibit signs of Vanity," offered Rev. Benny, an acknowledged authority on the Seven Deadly Sins. "He's probably in there admiring himself in the mirror."

"Okay, I'll go get him," sighed Richard. He opened the bedroom door and stepped inside. "Tommy, are you ready to play poker?" he was heard saying. Pause. Then came a shrill scream.

"What the hell?" exclaimed the elderly Wallowicz.

"Jesus," said Rev. Benny.

Richard Starkwell stumbled out of the bedroom, clutching his heart, face pale. "Ohmygod," he shouted. "Tommy is dead."

"Was it a heart attack?" asked Toby Newcastle.

"No, he's been stabbed."

"T-that's impossible," stammered the judge. "No one has been in that bedroom but Tommy. We were all out here the whole time."

"That's true," stated Daniel Wallowicz. "We were waiting for Richard to arrive."

"Guess you all have an alibi," said Four Fingers. "Alright if I phone Police Chief Johnny Leigh and tell him he's got a murder on his hands?"

"Yes, do that," said Richard. "Tell him to get down here right away."

Four Fingers looked at the stricken men. "Somebody oughta go confirm that Thomas Starkwell is dead," he said. "Make sure we don't need an ambulance too."

"Uh, I'm not comfortable with dead bodies," said the judge.

"Me neither," echoed the city commissioner.

"Dear me, I don't know how to do CPR," added the pastor.

"My heart might be able to take it," muttered the elderly real estate mogul.

"My only brother – " sobbed Richard. "I can't bear to look at him laying there dead."

Four Fingers said, "Okay, one of you call the police chief. I'll go check for a pulse."

He stepped into the bedroom and looked around. Nothing fancy, just a king-size bed, mirrored dresser, and writing table with a high-backed chair. Thomas Starkwell lay on the floor with a knife protruding from his chest. The blood wasn't flowing, which meant his heart had stopped pumping, but the former homicide detective felt his neck for a pulse anyway. Nothing.

Quickly examining the body, he noted no signs of a struggle. The clothing wasn't ripped, nothing out of place.

No furniture tipped over. No skin under the fingernails. No bruises on the skin. No defensive wounds.

That meant someone he knew and trusted likely killed him. One of the guys outside this room. But were they *all* lying – some sort of group cover-up? He could believe that of Wolloweicz and Newcastle, but of not a distinguished circuit court judge and a respected minister.

He searched the body, careful not to touch the knife. A calfskin wallet containing $500 was still in Thomas Starkwell's hip pocket; a Rolex remained on his wrist. So it didn't appear to be a robbery.

The closet door stood open. Empty except for wooden coat hangers.

The large plate glass window was latched, no indication of a forced entry.

No place for an assailant to hide.

A classic locked room mystery, he told himself. Even if the bedroom door hadn't actually been locked. Ruth Rendell or Agatha Christie would appreciate the challenge.

Four Fingers heard a knock at the bedroom door. "Johnny Leigh's here," called Rev. Benny. That was fast.

When he stepped back into the living room he was surprised by the police chief's casual appearance. Plaid Bermuda shorts and a T-shirt that said IF AT FIRST YOU DON'T SUCCEED, RELOAD AND TRY AGAIN. "I was having dinner down the street at Red Fish, Blue Fish when I got your call," he explained. Obviously feeling a little awkward being at a murder scene without his uniform.

"Somebody killed my brother," blurted Richard Starkwell. "Stabbed him in the heart."

"You're sure he's dead?"

"He's dead as a run-over iguana," replied Four Fingers. "You'll find him there in the bedroom."

"Any idea who did it?"

"None," said Judge Barbareau.

"It's a mystery," affirmed Rev. Benny Willingham. "Nobody went into that bedroom but Tommy Starkwell."

"That's right. We all have alibi," Toby Newcastle was quick to point out. He was coming up for reelection in a few months and didn't need any bad press. "We were all out here together. Well, everybody except Richard.

"Hey, I have an alibi," stated Richard Starkwell, chin held high. "I was with Four Fingers."

"That's true," said Wharton "Four Fingers" Dalessandro. "But he still killed his brother."

"W-what? You're accusing me? I've been with you all afternoon."

"Yeah, you're clever."

"Did you see him do it?" asked Johnny Leigh.

"No, but the answer's simple," smiled Four Fingers. "These guys are telling the truth. Nobody went into the bedroom ... except Richard when he found the body. So that means he had to have stabbed his brother just as he walked into the room, then claimed to have discovered him there on the floor."

"What was the motive?" asked the police chief. "They were brothers."

"So was Cain and Abel. Probably some dispute over a land deal. These guys would know better'n me."

"I did hear Thomas wanted to back out of that development deal on the navy land down near

Southernmost Point," Judge J. Randall Barbareau spoke up.

"Yes, I heard that too," said Daniel Wallowicz.

"The stupid fool, backing out would have cost us millions," growled Richard Starkwell, his anger showing.

"There you have it, everything but the confession."

"Yes, I did it. My brother was getting cold feet. If I didn't stop him, the navy deal would've fallen through. Southernmost Point is the perfect place for a casino. Plenty of parking over there behind Bahama Village."

"Sorry, Mr. Starkwell, I'm gonna have to take you in," said Johnny Leigh. "But I expect your friends here will have you out by morning."

Richard Starkwell turned to the man with the missing finger. "What made you suspicious of me?"

"Wasn't no other possibility. Besides, your inviting me to play poker with you big boys was just too unlikely. Made me suspicious that something was up. Turns out, you wanted me as your alibi, testifying I'd been with you non-stop all afternoon. You knew Johnny Leigh would believe me when I said you hadn't been outta my sight."

"Except for when he stepped into the bedroom and found his brother dead," the police chief completed the scenario.

"Yeah, dead about ten seconds after he entered that room."

"Well, you did solved another one," the police chief congratulated him. "Sure, you don't want that job as my chief homicide detective?"

"I'd rather keep painting houses."

"Not a very reliable profession," said Johnny Leigh.

"Why d'you say that?"

"Can't imagine Mr. Starkwell's gonna pay you after you busted him for murder."

"Aw crap. It's hard to make an honest living in this town."

"Guess that's why I have a job," nodded the lawman.

9

Four Fingers
And the Sinking Sun

Mallory Square is the site for Key West's famous Sunset Celebration, a daily Fellini-esque ritual designed for tourists. Throngs of cruise ship passengers and vacationers who have driven down from Ohio (and like wintery environs) enjoy applauding the setting sun while watching tightrope walkers, dog acts, escape artists, bagpipe players, trained domestic cats, magicians, and comedy routines on the wharf.

One tourist who liked this spectacle asked a policeman how many times a day it took place – this Sunset Celebration.

Wharton "Four Fingers" Dalessandro avoided this zoo whenever he could. But making his living as a housepainter, his latest job put him in the midst of all the craziness. A small building adjacent to Mallory Square served as an office for the Landlubbers Foundation, a non-profit group dedicated to protecting shorelines. The building's yellow paint was starting to peel like a banana.

Four Fingers worked with an outfit called Pretty As Paint, started up by a gay activist from Washington DC who had retired to Key West after a four-car traffic accident left him paralyzed from the waist down. He could manage crews of housepainters from his wheelchair.

By actual count, Four Fingers had live in this southernmost city in the continental US for seventeen years now. As the book said, *Quit Your Job and Move to Key West.* He mainly lived on his pension as a retired NYC homicide cop. The painting gig gave him something to do when he wasn't drinking beer, playing chess with his pal Dunk, or occasionally helping Police Chief Johnny Leigh solve crimes.

He and the young police chief got along fine, not that they were buds who hung out together. Word of his high clearance rate while working for New York's Finest had followed him south. Johnny kept trying to hire him, but Four Fingers didn't want real job.

He hadn't been called Four Fingers when he arrived in the so-called Conch Republic, but a fishing accident took his index finger, leaving him with a new nickname. Who wanted to catch a giant marlin anyway?

That morning as Four Fingers and his fellow painters propped up their ladders and opened paint cans and checked their camelhair brushes, he recognized a familiar face walking across the nearly empty square. Bill Buttonwood had been a bank robber who shot his partner during an argument over the spoils. Wharton Dalessandro had helped send him up for ten to twenty.

He watched as the skinny man paused at an open-air tourist bar and bought a novelty drink, rum and coconut water in the shell. Must be flush to be buying an overpriced tourist drink like that, $15 a pop at Coconut

Tom's Rum Shack. People from northern climes thought it was island-y to drink from a real coconut.

"Excuse me, guys," he said to the crew. "Back in five."

He climbed down the aluminum ladder and walked across the red brick to where Buttonwood stood sipping rum through a straw from the green coconut. Early in the day for drinking, but some people required a non-stop transfusion of alcohol.

The thin man looked up, narrowed his green eyes, and lowered his coconut. "I'll be damned. Is that you, Lieutenant Dalessandro?"

Four Fingers offered a grim smile. "You can drop the lieutenant. I'm long retired."

"Me too."

"When did you get out?" Sing Sing had been the man's home last time Four Fingers had seen the convicted murderer. He'd been working in the laundry. Not a big change since Buttonwood had owned a dry cleaning service before turning to bank robbery.

"Couple of years now. I kinda miss it. Three squares a day, a roof over my head."

"What you doing now?"

"That's the problem. Nothing. Came down to Key West to change my luck."

"Want a job on a paint crew?"

The man's jaw dropped. "You'd hire me?"

"Why not? You served your time."

"Hell, yeah."

"Come here at 8 a.m. tomorrow morning. I'll arrange things with the boss."

"Thanks. Just blew my last dollar on this coconut."

"Where's your suitcase?"

"I'm traveling light. Clothes on my back."

Four Fingers eyed the expensive Egyptian cotton trousers, the hand-stitched shirt with a fleur-de-lis design. Not bad clothes for a hobo. But the man looked hungry nonetheless. "Here's five bucks. Go get some breakfast. There's a Wendy's about four blocks up Duval."

"Thanks," Bill Buttonwood said. He started to leave, then did a Columbo. "Just for the record, I didn't shoot my partner back then. Arnie Ferguson did it. The three of us were arguing over the split."

Four Fingers narrowed his eyes, frowned. "Stow it, Bill. I don't rehash old cases."

"How about new ones?"

"What d'you mean?"

"I know where there's a dead body."

"You kill him?"

"No," snorted Bill Buttonwood. "I stumbled across the body last night while looking for a place to crash."

"And you didn't report it?"

"That's likely to happen – a convicted murderer phoning in a report about a dead Cuban."

"A Cuban? You sure about that?"

"Direct from Havana. Came ashore yesterday afternoon."

"Where'd you find him?" Four Fingers asked, pulling out his ancient Nokia to phone the police chief.

"Underneath the White Street Pier. That's where they set off the Fourth of July fireworks, ain't it?"

Four Fingers nodded. "Let's go see your Cuban."

"Is there a reward for this?"

"Not up to me. I'm a civilian, remember? I paint houses."

They walked up to the Hog's Breath Saloon, where they found Dunk Reid nursing a beer at the bar beneath the shade of a large tree. On the tiny stage, a country western singer was picking at his guitar and moaning about blue eyes crying in the rain, a passible imitation of Willy Nelson. Dunk finished his beer and led them to his battered pickup truck parked on Front Street. "You'd think I was a taxi service," he grumbled.

The sun was in their eyes as the pickup bounced along the potholes on South Street. An orange sign said ROADWORK, but there were no workers in sight. Palm trees advertised the tropical climate, like pictures from a slick travel brochure. But the red frangipani and purple bougainvillea flowers along the road were wilting in the morning's heat.

"This place always this hot?" complained Bill Buttonwood. Dunk's pickup had no air-conditioning. A tiny battery-operated fan was mounted on the dashboard, but it barely stirred the thick air.

"You get used to it," said Four Fingers. "Better'n snow."

Swinging past the monolith of the Casa Marina Hotel, they could see the beach. Volleyball players were jumping about like marionettes, smacking a ball across a sagging net. Picnickers were spreading food on concrete tables sheltered under tin roofs. The redbrick walls of the Garden Club loomed ahead of them, the remnant of a crumbling Civil War fort.

Police Chief Johnny Leigh was waiting for them at White Street Pier. He wore his starched uniform, silver badge flashing in the bright morning sunlight like a signal mirror. "We located the body," he greeted them. "Wedged pretty far up under the pier. Couldn't hardly see it until we waded in."

"We?" muttered his sergeant, uniform soaked.

"Right where your guy said it would be," Johnny Leigh continued, ignoring the comment. He eyed the skinny guy in the ivory-colored outfit standing next to Dunk's truck. He could recognize a prison pallor when he saw one.

"Was it a Cuban?" asked Four Fingers.

"Can't tell till we pull the body out. My forensic boys are on the way. Don't want to disturb the crime scene till they get here."

Four Fingers shrugged. "In the meantime, you can arrest Bill Buttonwood here for the murder."

"Hey!" shouted the man. "What's going on? Are you trying to pin this on me?"

"Yep. No question you did it, Bill. Anymore than there was a question last time I nailed you."

"That was back then – "

"And this is now. You couldn't have stumbled across this dead man last night, him stuck back under the pier outta sight. You had to have had a hand in putting him there. Besides, you not only knew he was from Cuba, but that he'd come over from Havana yesterday. How'd you know that stuff if he was already dead when you found him?"

"Well, uh – "

"You and your partner robbed and killed him, then hid the body."

"Partner? What partner?"

"I'd guess Arnie Ferguson. You and he went up the river together. Prison time probably made you two close."

"Wasn't anybody else involved," scoffed Bill Buttonwood.

"You couldn't have done it alone.'

"Why not?"

"You'd have had to get pretty wet stashing that body under the pier. And you told me the clothes on your back are all you've got. Those cotton trousers would've shrunk to the size of kid's underpants if you'd worn them into the water."

"I took them off."

"Ha! There's your confession, chief. I don't know if he had a partner or not. Just wanted to back him into a corner."

"So I shouldn't bother putting an APB out on this Arnie Ferguson?"

"Naw, he died in prison from a fungus infection. Guess Bill didn't hear about that."

The police chief shook his head, amazed at the quick solution. "Why'd he tell you about the dead man in the first place?" he wanted to know.

"Bragging. I sent him away for murder once. He wanted to flaunt this latest crime in front of me, me not knowing he was guilty. A chance to prove he was smarter than the guy who caught him the first time."

"Guess that didn't work out," said Johnny Leigh as he snapped the metal cuffs onto the gaunt man's wrists.

Arching an eyebrow, Four Fingers twisted his face into a Robert De Niro squint. "Billy Boy might've had me if he hadn't denied committing that first murder. But I knew he was guilty – seven witnesses. So I wondered what else he might be lying about. Like stumbling across a drowned Cuban, a Wet-Foot Dry-Foot gone bad."

Bill Buttonwood angrily spat on the ground. The sand was so hot the spittle sizzled. "Damn my luck, bumping into *you* in this end-of-the-road town, Wharton Dalessandro."

"Good to see you too," said Four Fingers. "But can I have my five bucks back? The jail over on Stock Island will serve you breakfast for free."

10

Four Fingers
And Fat Aloysius

Fat Aloysius could usually be found on a barstool at the Red Macaw. Actually, two barstools. His 300-pound girth spilled over. He preferred drinking rum straight up. He could easily hold two-dozen drinks at a sitting without showing any sign of intoxication. His day job had strict office hours, between 10 and 3 p.m. He was a bookie.

Clients wafted into the Red Macaw like apparitions, handed him a slip of paper, then left. They never stayed to have a drink with him. These bets were settled up each Friday, after people had cashed their paychecks.

The bartenders at the Red Macaw knew Fat Aloysius's occupation. Hell, they placed bets with him too. But tradition said they turned a blind eye to his slightly illegal activities. Rumor was the bar's proprietors got a cut of the action.

According to some historians, the Red Macaw is the second oldest saloon in Key West. The bar claimed Harry S. Truman had been a patron whenever he visited the Little White House. A framed photograph over the bar did picture the 33rd president of the United States knocking back a shot of whiskey on the premises.

Wharton "Four Fingers" Dalessandro was not a client of Fat Aloysius. He didn't gamble on football games, horse races, or local elections. He played chess with his pal Dunk Reid for $10 a game, but Fat Aloysius didn't handicap such matches. That's why the barflies were surprised to see Four Fingers walk into the Red Macaw, hand the big man a slip of paper, then leave.

And so Police Chief Johnny Leigh called him back to the Red Macaw an hour later when Fat Aloysius turned up dead. The bookie's oversized body had been found in the men's room, throat cut. "You were his last customer," explained the young lawman.

"Not me," Four Fingers shook his head. He was still dressed in his work clothes, paint-splattered Bermuda shorts and a T-shirt that could have passed as tie-dyed. A duck-billed fishing cap covered his graying hair. There was a speck of dried white paint on his left cheek.

"C'mon, there are two dozen witnesses," Johnny Leigh pointed out, surprised by the response. He looped dapper in his starched blue uniform by contrast. He displayed a 9mm Glock on his belt and a shiny badge on his breast pocket.

"Oh, I was here. But not to place a bet."

"The bartender saw you pass him a slip of paper."

"Sure, but it wasn't a bet." Four Fingers gave the bartender a glare. Tom Finnegan averted his eyes, busying himself slicing limes at the far end of the long mahogany bar.

The police chief smirked. "Don't tell me you were slipping him your phone number?" Everybody knew Fat

Aloysius was gay as a goose. He lived with a drag queen who worked at the 801 Club.

"Jealous?" laughed Four Fingers. Johnny Leigh was long out of the closet, not that anybody noticed in this rainbow-friendly community.

"I'm trying to solve a murder here."

"Fat Aloysius wanted to get his house painted. I was merely delivering a quote from Ronnie." Ronnie Milsap (no relation to the singer) was the owner of Pretty As Paint, the company that Four Fingers worked for when he felt inclined to work.

"Strange, he didn't have that on his person when we searched his body."

"What *did* you find?"

"Half a dozen bet slips. A wad of cash – close to ten grand. Car keys that fit that big orange Hummer he drives. Drivers license, no wallet. He never carries one. Twenty-three cents in change."

"But no quote for painting his house."

"Nope."

Four Fingers scratched his head in puzzlement. His hair was salt-and-pepper, bespeaking his 57 years. "It was a pretty good price; I don't think he would've thrown it away."

"Since you're here, d'you want to lend a hand with this case?" Police Chief Johnny Leigh knew that Wharton Dalessandro had spent twenty years with the New York Police Department, a lieutenant in the homicide Division when he retired. On occasion he'd assisted the Key West police in solving a murder. Only last month he'd fingered (pardon the pun) the man who killed a boat captain named Long John Silber.

"Gee, Johnny, you oughta have this one figured out," Four Fingers told the lawman.

"How so? He had six bets on him, making each of them a suspect."

"Those guys didn't do it. Their bets were too fresh to have any results. So no sour grapes, money owed, or hard feelings – yet. Beside, they made their bets and left with Fat Aloysius still alive here on the bar stool."

"Then one of his old bets?"

"Maybe. But since he got murdered in the restroom, the killer had to be someone inside the bar at that time."

"That means the killer's still here. The minute the bartender discovered the body in the men's room, he locked the doors and called the police."

"Did you find the knife?"

"Yeah, it was laying on the restroom floor." He reached into a large bag that looked like it was made for pizza delivery and pulled out a Ziploc bag containing a wide-bladed ginsu knife. "*Voila*," he said.

"I didn't know you spoke French."

"In more ways than one," he quipped. "Does this knife help you identify the murderer?"

"I think I've got it figured out. But one more question."

"Yeah?"

"Did you find Fat Aloysius's ledger book?"

"Ledger book?"

"Where he keeps track of who he owes money and who owes him money."

"No. Why's that important?

Four Fingers pointed to the bar's cash register, but he had to use his left hand. His right index finger was missing from a fishing accident – hence his nickname. "Bet you'll find the ledger book in the cash register under the money tray. And it will show that Tom Fennigan owed Fat Aloysius a bundle."

"Tom the bartender?"

"That's be my hunch. Tom was here everyday with the fat man, was a regular customer. He was the one who found the body, maybe killed him just prior to 'discovering' him."

"Clifford, keep your eye on Tom," said the police chief.

"Careful, Chief. He's accusing Tom based on some pretty thin guesswork."

"A little more than that."

"Oh, what?"

"That ginsu knife is just like the one Tom was using to slice limes a minute ago. They usually come in a set. Bet Tom has one missing – the one in your bag. Nobody else would've had access to them, for he keeps the cutlery behind the bar where no one else is allowed."

"Tom, could I talk with you?" called Johnny Leigh.

"Aw, crap. Why did you have to call Four Fingers Dalessandro in on this? I coulda got away with it."

"I can understand why Tom took the ledger," said the sergeant, fishing it out of the cash drawer. "He wanted to destroy any record of his gambling debt. Says here he owed more'n two grand. A hefty sum for a bartender. But why'd he take your Pretty As Paint bid?" He held up the slip of paper that he found alongside the ledger.

"Simple. He was doing his brother a favor."

"Jimmy Finnegan?"

"Jimmy owns Brilliant Brushes, the main competitor to Pretty As Paint. Tom was trying to make sure Fat Aloysius's partner gave the job to his brother's company even with Fat Aloysius dead."

Johnny turned to the bartender. "That true, Tom?"

Tom Finnegan raised his chin defiantly. "Killing two birds with one stone, you might say."

"Now that Four Fingers has identified you as the culprit," said the police chief, "I doubt that Poison Polly is going to give that housepainting job to your brother."

"Oh, what the hell," shrugged the bartender. "At least I don't have to come up with the two grand."

11

Four Fingers
And the Free Beer

Whenever Wharton "Four Fingers" Dalessandro chose to work, he painted houses for Pretty As Paint, a local company owned by Ronnie Milsap (not *that* one). This Ronnie was a 300-pound blind albino who knew more about matching color schemes that most sighted paint store salesmen. Funny that he and the also-blind singer should have the same name.

Four Fingers lived off a small pension from twenty years with the New York police, so the housepainting was just a way to spent his time when not drinking beers or playing chess with his pal Dunk Reid.

Ronnie found that eyesight wasn't needed to schedules paint crews. Since most of his customers lived in the Old Town Historic district, the choice of exterior colors was limited by the Historic Architecture Review Commission (HARC). Trick was matching wall colors with the color of shutters. "It's not rocket science," said Ronnie, who used to work in Cape Canaveral on NASA's Space Program before losing his eyesight in a traffic accident. Who would have thought a third-of-a-ton man could get thrown through a VW's windshield?

Settling in Key West, Ronnie took up his father's trade,

one he'd worked in all way through college. Yes, he came from a long line of housepainters. His great-great grandfather had painted the Pink House in Silvermine, CT, where George Washington was claimed to have slept.

Dunk Reid found Four Fingers having a beer at Irish Kevin's. It wasn't a bar he usually frequented, its clientele being mainly tourists doing the Duval Crawl. He liked the fact that Irish Kevin sat on the stage with his guitar, calling out through the open-front bar to passersby on the street, luring them inside. And when he asked the uninitiated visitors where they were from, if the answer was "New York," his audience was trained to shout, "Fuck You!"

Rude, but fun.

"Whatzup?" asked Four Fingers, looking up from his Beamish Irish Stout. A dark and chocolaty beer, it features a lighter body and spicier bite than Guinness.

"Ronnie Milsap's been arrested," Dunk shouted in his ear, trying to compete with the high-decibel amps that broadcast Irish Kevin's songs throughout the cavernous bar.

"For what? Crossing on a red light?"

"They're saying he murdered Stinking Alfred Barnsworth." Stinking Al was one of the painters on Crew Number Two, the one Four Fingers usually worked with. He knew Stinking Al pretty well, a former Wall Street trader who'd suffered a mental breakdown and had been found wandering the streets in Key West. How he got there, nobody knows. Ronnie had given him a job to get him out of the homeless shelter. Stinking Al had been renting a room in back of the Pretty As Paint offices on Bertha Street.

Four Fingers stood up and followed Dunk to the sidewalk where the music wasn't as loud. "How Sinking Al get killed?"

"Maisy the cleaning lady found the body in Ronnie's locked office last night. And Ronnie's the only one with a key. Al had been brained in the head with a gallon can of Benjamin Moore Eggshell White."

"Guess I better go talk with Police Chief Johnny Leigh." Four Fingers and Johnny were buds of sorts. Not that they drank beer together. But he'd on occasion helped the young lawman solve a crime. A habit from his old days on the NYPD.

"He's probably still at the crime scene. Minute I heard about it, I hotfooted it over here to Duval Street looking for you." Dunk Reid was born on the island, a full-fledged fifth-generation Conch. The coconut telegraph seemed to run through his living room in that big Victorian house on Eaton that he'd inherited (along with a trust fund) from his father.

"Let's go."

When Dunk's battered blue pickup skidded to a stop in front of the Pretty As Pain building, the police chief's cruiser was still parked in front along with two other police cars that had blue lights pulsing on their roofs. Yellow crime scene tape already barred the front door. Several members of the paint crews lingered outside, talking in low voices, worried about whether they would be out of jobs with Ronnie Milsap behind bars.

"Hey, Land Shark, what are they saying?" four fingers called to one of the painters.

"That Ronnie hadda do it. Nobody else had access to

that office where they found Sinking Al."

"Any sign of a break-in?"

"Not according to the police." Four Fingers knew that Land Shark McGurty's brother was a sergeant on the force, so he'd have an inside track.

Four Fingers walked over to the door blocked by the yellow tape. The pink building was a converted garage consisting of an office, two storage rooms (one for paint; the other for such equipment as brushes and pails and aluminum ladders), a cramped restroom, and a large open space with a card table where the painters hung out between jobs. The cop inside the door nodded at him in recognition and said, "Just a minute."

When he came back, he pulled the yellow tape aside and said, "Chief says for you to come in."

Four fingers slipped inside the darkened building. Too much CSI television where cops walk around in the dark with flashlights. How were you supposed to see a clue in the dark? "Hi Johnny. Ronnie still here?"

"He's sitting in a police van out the back. We're waiting for the coroner. He was having a Cuban sandwich at El Siboney and refused to come till he'd finished eating."

"A little late for lunch."

"You've seen the coroner. Tubby Thompson makes Ronnie look downright skinny. I think he eats ten meals a day."

Four Fingers glanced about the familiar surroundings. Nothing out of place. Paint mixer in the corner. A Marilyn Monroe calendar (a reproduction of the Tom Kelly nude) was tacked to the restroom door. A deck scattered haphazardly on the surface of the card table. "Has Ronnie confessed?"

"Said he didn't do it."

"Hmm, can I see the body?"

"Sure, but hold your nose. Stinking Al lives up to his name." The little man was known for his body order, hence the nickname. He never bathed because he believed microscopic aliens invaded our bodies through tap water – refuges from Mars because the water there had dried up.

Stepping into the office, Four Fingers spotted the body on the floor behind the desk. He could have found it with his eyes closed. The dead man looked like a pile of *ropa vieja*, old clothes. A paint-stained T-shirt, unzipped Bermuda shorts, a bullet hole in the center of his pallid forehead. "Where's the gun?" asked the sometimes housepainter.

"Here," said Johnny Leigh, holding up a Ziploc bag containing a dainty little .22, an Ivor Johnson revolver.

Four Fingers bent over to look in the wastepaper basket. "Hmm, what's this?"

"Just some tin foil. Probably a candy wrapper. My guys didn't see any connection."

"Where's Maisy Ridenour?"

Johnny Leigh shrugged, his badge flashing in the overhead light. "The cleaning lady who found the body? We let her go after taking a statement. She's easy to find. Lives over on Eisenhower."

"Better go pick her up," said Four Fingers. "She did it, not Ronnie."

The police chief looked nonplussed. "How d'you figure that. Wharton?"

"Pretty simple. Ronnie Milsap couldn't have shot

Stinking Al. He's blind as a bat – and that shot was square in the middle of Al's forehead like a Buddha third eye. Good aim. That leaves Maisy."

"Ronnie could have pressed the gun against his head by touch."

"No powder burns. Wasn't a close-up shot."

"Okay – but why her?"

"You found Stinking Al in a locked office. Only Ronnie had a key, I was told. But that's not true. Maisy the cleaning lady had one too. How else could she have got into the office to do the cleaning ... or find the body?"

"Why would she kill Al?"

"Probably a lover's quarrel. She saw him all the time, her coming around after hours to clean, Al living in that shed out back. They probably came in here to have sex on Ronnie's desk. A neatfreak like Maisy never would've wanted to meet in Al's smelly shambles of a room."

"Yucko – those two having sex?"

"Yep. Al's pants are unzipped. And that tin foil in the trashcan's from a condom wrapper. Use that brand myself."

"So where's the condom?"

"Look on Al's dick. The coroner would've found it."

"You're sure about this?"

"One other thing. That cute little .22 is a lady's handgun. It would've been lost in Ronnie's big meathooks. He owned a hefty .45 Colt. Showed it to me once. You'll probably find it at his apartment."

"Damn, Wharton. Looks like you just saved your job."

"Don't tell Ronnie. He'd think it was a reward to give me more hours with a paintbrush. Don't wanna work that hard."

12
Four Fingers
And the Bad Czech

Wharton "Four Fingers" Dalessandro was walking down Truman Avenue, the street that divides the island in half. In the early days of Key West it was actually called Division Street. He was reminiscing about the used bookstore across the street, the one that had closed leaving the building strewn with paperback books, scrap paper, and a few empty cardboard boxes.

Suddenly a naked blonde threw herself into his arms. "Help!" she screamed into Four Finger's ear. Her 36C's pressed against him like twin water balloons. They felt good enough to be real – a testimonial for the pliancy of silicon.

"Whoa, lady," he said, pushing her away. But not immediately. "You seem to have lost your clothes."

"No, I work in there," she pointed at the boxy two-story building with the neon sign proclaiming GIRLS GIRLS GIRLS. The locals called it Girls, although its official name was Naked Bunch.

Four Fingers studied her blonde pixie cut, plastic boobs, rounded hips, slender legs. Certainly worth a few twenties thrown onto a stage. "Uh, what are you doing out here then?"

"A dead man," she moaned, looking over her shoulder as if a ghost might be pursuing her from the Girls building. The parking lot was empty, and likely so was Girls. It was not yet 8 in the morning, the sun an orange glow in the eastern sky.

"Dead?"

"The owner," she hiccupped. Her mascara was starting to run. She had a slight accent, probably Czechoslovakian. Without pretty Czech girls the island would have fewer waitresses and strippers. They came over on temporary visas, worked, and sent money back home.

"D'you mean Edgar Stoneman?" He was the richer-than-Croesus Texas oilman who'd bought Naked Bunch last year. He'd taken it from a pasties-and-G-string club to an All Nude sex emporium.

"Y-yes, Mr. Stoney Man. That's who is dead."

Four Fingers peeled off his T-shirt, the one that said SHIT CREEK SURVIVOR and slipped it over her head. It covered her like a short, white dress. "Let's go check on your boss."

"O-okay."

The interior of Naked Bunch was dark and silent. Chairs were upended on tables. The stage and its runway were empty. A neon sign advertised CORONA with a bright red glow over the bar.

"Hello, anybody here?" shouted Four Fingers, forming a megaphone with his cupped hands. The girl huddled at his side. The air conditioning wasn't running. His bare chest was sweaty in the heat.

No answer.

"Is there anybody here besides you and Mr. Stoneman?" he asked.

"N-no. Mr. Stoney Man asked me to meet him here this morning. But he dead when I got here." She struggled to hold back the tears, button nose quivering.

"Where is the late Mr. Stoneman."

"He was not late. Mr. Stoney Man got here before me."

Four Fingers rolled his eyes. "I mean, where's the dead body."

"Over there," she indicated the bar.

He walked over to the polished mahogany bar and peered over it. There on the floor, in the red glare of the CORONA sign lay a man with a knife protruding from his back. Sure looked dead.

"We better call the police," he said.

"No police please. I have not a permit to work."

"Sorry, honey. But we've got a murder here." He reached for the black telephone on a shelf behind the bar. He knew the direct line of Police Chief Johnny Leigh by heart. They had been friends ever since he landed in the Conch Republic some seventeen years ago, newly retire as a NYPD homicide detective.

Yes, he'd seen his share of dead bodies.

"Wait!" said the girl, tugging on his arm. "I will do anything you want if you do not make this phone call."

He turned to see that she'd stripped off his T-shirt, naked again. An open invitation. Tempting as it was, he shook his head, said "Sorry," and dialed the number.

By the time the Key West police arrived, the girl – she said her name was Tula – had dressed in her street clothes. Four Fingers sat beside her on a bar stool sipping a beer, his SHIT CREEK SURVIVOR T-shirt back on his brawny shoulders. He'd helped himself to the Red Stripe, figuring that the club owed him that much for making him late to work. Whenever the spirit moved him, he painted houses for an outfit called Pretty As Paint. Gave him something to do when he wasn't playing chess with his pal Dunk Reid.

"So what happened?" asked Police Chief Johnny Leigh. He was an olive-complexioned man in his late thirties, those sensitive brown doe-eyes belaying a tough-as-leather interior. He'd worked his way up from traffic cop to chief, not an easy task being that he was not only Hispanic but gay. But his men respected him, and Mayor Henry Kale backed him. Truth was, the mayor owed him big for pulling his daughter out of a scrape or two.

Four Fingers had already explained the part about the girl accosting him on the street and him discovering the dead owner inside the strip club. So the blonde pixie picked up the story from there. "Mr. Stoney Man, he asked me to meet him here this morning to do a bar inventory. When I arrived he was already expired."

"Was there anyone else here?"

"No. But as I ran outside to get help, I spied a bald man driving out of the parking lot in a yellow Florida Aqueduct truck. Do you think he killed Mr. Stoney Man?"

"Best suspect we got right now," said the Police Chief.

Four Fingers looked fidgety. "I've gotta get to work," he said. "We're prepping ol' Mr. McCourt's house today. That eyebrow house on Fleming. Go ahead and arrest Tula here, so I can get going."

"Arrest her?"

"She did it, killed her boss 'cause he was trying to have sex with her."

Johnny Leigh looked puzzled. But his sergeant – a big guy named Clifford Weeks – stepped in front of the door to make sure nobody left. Four Fingers wasn't sure whether it was him or the girl whose exit was being blocked. "How d'you figure all that?" asked the police chief.

"She's lying about him being dead when she got here, else how did she get in the club. Edgar Stoneman wasn't going to give keys to a Czech chick."

"Maybe he'd left the door unlocked because he'd been expected her to help him with the inventory?" tried the lawman.

"Tula here's a dancer, not a bartender. He wouldn't have asked a pole swinger to count liquor bottles."

"Maybe he was short handed."

"No, I'm short handed," said Four Fingers, holding up his right hand to illustrate his missing digit, an index finger lost in a fishing accident. Hence, his nickname. "Besides, she was stark naked when she came running out of the club. Not exactly the proper dress for taking inventory. Ol' Edgar was putting the moves on her. Had her meet him at the club this morning when nobody was there, got her naked, but she didn't go along with the program and stabbed him with a knife the bartender keeps back there for slicing lemons and limes. That big blade in Edgar's chest is not a fishing knife or the kind of pig-sticker someone carries around in his pocket."

"What about the guy in the Aqueduct van she saw?"

"Aw, she's lying about that. First of all, Aqueduct vans aren't yellow. Second, I was on the sidewalk outside when

111

she came running out of the club and I didn't see no van. And the only baldheaded man I've seen all morning is your guy Clifford over there."

"Hey –" objected the sergeant. He'd never been particularly fond of Four Fingers Dalessandro, always sticking his nose into police business.

"Please, Mr. Police Chief," said the dancer, "I didn't mean to kill him. But he was trying to rape me." A confession.

"Probably true," said the sergeant. "We've had complaints about Stoneman before. Treating his strippers like his own private harem."

Four Fingers shook his head, as if correcting a schoolchild with the wrong answer on a quiz. "More likely Tula led him on, got her boss to meet her here for sex, then stabbed him and took the cashbox with last night's receipts."

"So where's she hiding the cashbox?" snorted the sergeant, eyeing the girl's tight blouse and short shorts. Not even a purse in hand. "Up her –"

"Clifford!" Johnny Leigh cut him off. "Let Wharton answer the question."

"Check her locker backstage. When she got dressed she made me turn my back while she opened it. Since she was already naked, that seemed like unnecessary modesty less she was hiding something in that locker."

"Please, let me go," begged Tula. "If you do I will have sex with all of you." To show the sincerity of her offer, she unbuttoned her blouse exposing her surgically perfect breasts.

"Sorry, but you've got the wrong police chief," said Johnny Leigh. Whether he was referring to his integrity or to his sexual orientation wasn't quite clear.

"Uh, right," muttered the sergeant. Frowning.

"Not me either," said Wharton "Four Fingers" Dalessandro. "I'm already late for work."

13

Four Fingers and the Dead Drag Queen

Wharton "Four Fingers" Dalessandro hoisted the bottle of Red Stripe and chugalugged it. He was ready to go home to his cigar-maker's cottage on Olivia Street after an evening at the Schooner Wharf with his pal Dunk Reid. It wasn't hard to outdrink the diminutive islander, for at 5' 10" Four Fingers had a lot more body mass to absorb the alcohol than Dunk. Like a wizen leprechaun, Dunk would be lucky to hit 5' 2" in his stocking feet.

Not that the little man ever wore stockings, for the summer weather in Key West was just too hot, even with the sea breezes. Like most people who lived here, he wore boat shoes with no socks, baggy Bermuda shorts, and a colorful T-shirt. Today's tee offered A PENNY FOR YOUR THOUGHTS. A DOLLAR IF YOU FLASH ME!

Forget about the dollar. With New Year's Eve coming up, girls would unhesitatingly flash you for 10¢ worth of plastic beads.

Welcoming in the New Year was a big deal on Duval Street. Every year at the Bourbon Street Pub a drag queen known as Sushi dropped at Midnight in a giant papier-mâché slipper, spewing sparkling champagne from a bottle onto the cheering crowds. Guys in the hoard below were bare-chested, or wore chaps with buttocks showing, or displayed more tats that Ray Bradbury's Illustrated Man. The women were mostly blonde, sometimes with cowboy hats, necks laden with strands of cheap plastic beads, raising their T-shirts and blouses to display their boobs in return for more wampum.

Anderson Cooper and Kathy Griffith would cut from Times Square to Key West to check out what outrageous things Sushi might say this year. Like the time she stated that "Anderson Cooper is out and about," but the scene clicked off at "Anderson Cooper is out ..." That was before the silver-haired commentator officially came out of the closet. Sushi took a little heat for that, not that it bothered her.

Dunk and Four Fingers usually spent their New Year's on the other side of the island, at the Bight where the Schooner Wharf Bar lowered a pirate wench at Midnight. Yo ho ho.

Not that they didn't enjoy Sushi's outrageous antics, but there was a loyalty owed to the Schooner Wharf because the proprietors let them play chess on the premises every afternoon. After the chess game, the guys might linger for a bite of dinner, maybe even enjoy a few bottles of beer. After all this time at the bar they knew the words to entertainer Michael McCloud's songs better than he did.

McCloud was the island's answer to Jimmy Buffett, who had abandoned Key West after becoming famous, leaving his Margaritaville bar behind as a memento. McCloud was famous for writing the Conch Republic

National Anthem, a paean to leaving northern cold weather behind. The Conch Republic is another name for Key West, a holdover from those drug-running days when bales of square grouper (i.e. marijuana) floated ashore nightly.

That was long before Four Fingers came to Key West, to embrace a sedate existence as a sometimes housepainter, after twenty years as a homicide dick with the NYPD. He'd been down here seventeen years, but still couldn't get over the fact that he was now living in Paradise.

His pal Dunk was a true Key Wester, the man's family going back five generations on the island. That made him a Conch (pronounced "konk"), a status only birth could bestow. Dunk's father had been a burly man who once arm-wrestled Ernest Hemingway and fished for giant marlin with the great writer back in the '30s. Right after that Hemingway became a war correspondent, derisively called "Ernie Hemorrhoid," a play on the name of that other great contemporary journalist, Ernie Pyle. After that, Hemingway migrated to Cuba with his new lady friend, leaving his Key West compound to become a tourist attraction.

Being a Conch, Dunk Reid had more relatives than Biblical Adam. He was always introducing people as "my cousin" to Four Fingers. That's why tonight while Four Fingers chugalugged his last beer before heading home, he didn't think much about the man who slipped onto a barstool next to him. The gaunt scarecrow had been introduced to him as "Cousin Raf."

Raf – short for Rafael – was Dunk's mother's sister's boy, a 38-year-old ne'er-do-well who sometimes worked as a shrimper. An uncut shock of sandy hair made his narrow face appear even slimmer. His clothes looked dirty, his unwashed feet encased in untied boat shoes. He held up a Marlboro, a cig he'd obviously bummed off someone.

"Got a light, man?"

"Don't smoke," replied Four Fingers. "But that cigar roller over there will let you use his torch." A dark-haired Cuban set up shop every night at Schooner Wharf, rolling cigars made with "100% Cuban-seed tobacco."

"Can you lend me twenty dollars?"

Four Fingers grunted a *no*. "Ask your cousin over here," he nodded toward Dunk, who was all but head-on-the-bar drunk.

"No way," mumbled Dunk, shooing away the request with a wave of his free hand; the other one clutching a Budweiser. "Raf still owes me ten dollars from last week."

"Hey, I'll pay you back outta the twenty."

"Oh, okay," hiccupped Dunk. Four Fingers rolled his eyes as the inebriated little man peeled off a twenty from his roll and handed it to his cousin. "Now gimme my ten," demanded Dunk.

"You got change?"

"Sure, here." Dunk passed him two tens and the man handed one back – now in possession of the original twenty plus the ten.

"Thanks, cousin," said Raf.

"Don't mention it."

Four Fingers was pretty sure Raf wouldn't mention it, hoping that Dunk was too drunk to remember the exchange. "I'm heading home," he said, sliding his butt off the barstool. The sand under his feet seemed a little unsteady.

"Fore you go, wanna see a dead man?"

He turned to the slender man. "Who's dead?" The old cop juices bubbling in his brain.

"Dunno. Some tourist I think. Gilded Glenda showed him to me a few minutes ago. Out there in the back alley behind the bandstand."

Gilded Glenda (né Harvey Milnik) was a drag queen known for her penchant for gold lamé gowns. She worked her way from bar to bar, dancing for tourists in return for drinks – the later the evening, the wilder her terpsichorean antics.

"Better show me," said Four Fingers.

"Cost you twenty dollars."

Without hesitating, Four Fingers forked over the portrait of Alexander Hamilton. "Let's go see the dead man."

Raf led him and Dunk to the back of the bar, a dusty street barely wide enough for a beer delivery truck. Tonight it was clogged with parked cars – two rusty Jeeps, an old VW, a Ford with a cracked windshield, and a shiny Hummer. "Dead guy's in that Hummer. Pecked on his window to borrow a dollar for a beer when I noticed he had a big ol' knife sticking in his chest."

"Where does Gilded Glenda come in?"

"Oh, she was sitting in the Hummer beside the dead man. Man, her makeup was a mess. Mascara running down her cheeks. Hair looked like a bird's nest."

"Where's Glenda now?"

"Who knows? She bolted when she saw me at the window. Jumped out of that big-ass vehicle an' run like a ghost was chasing her."

Four Fingers walked around to the driver's side, peered in the open window. Sure enough, a slender knife like you use to filet fish was protruding awkwardly from the man's chest. Eyes closed, mouth open, his face had achieved a pale yellowish cast in death. He wore an expensive Tommy Bahama shirt, pressed slacks with unzipped fly, Nike running shoes. An open red-and-white pack of Marlboros was balanced on the tan dashboard above the steering wheel. The registration in the glove box identified him as Roger Allen Willard of Valdosta, Georgia. The Hummer bore that out with a Georgia license plate.

"Yep, looks like a tourist all right. Johnny Leigh's not going to be very happy about this." The police chief's main imperative was to prevent visitors from getting harmed – tourism being the backbone of the island's economy. Under Chief Leigh's so-far eight-year term, murders had declined 27%. Petty burglaries were up 4%, but no one cared about that.

"Hey, I'm not hanging around for the police. I'll bid you gentlemen goodnight. You two can play Good Citizen and call it in. Just don't mention my name."

"Can't do that," said Four Fingers.

"Why not?"

"'Cause you killed ol' Roger Willard here. Gilded Glenda will confirm that when we find her."

"Well, then I'm walking, cause you ain't gonna find that crossdressing bitch. She's gone for good."

"Oh? Where did you put her body?"

"Huh?"

"Here's what happened: Glenda was giving this tourist a blowjob in his Hummer – no pun intended. His fly's open. You came along and stabbed him for his fat wallet, then offed Glenda because she witnessed the whole thing."

"No, it happened like I told you."

"Couldn't have. You said you knocked on the window, but as you can see it's open. A dead man couldn't have rolled it down."

"Maybe Gilded Glenda rolled it down."

"You said she bolted. No time to fiddle with the window. Glenda's nervous and high-strung; she wouldn't have been sitting here in this vehicle alone with a dead man. She only ran when you stabbed her john."

"How d'you know *she* didn't put the knife in him?" Raf was looking panicky, like he was about to cut and run. But Dunk held onto his arm, a flimsy restrain given the little man's inebriated condition.

"By its angle in his chest. He was stabbed through the open window."

"Damn. Guess I may as well admit it. Glenda's dead too. She grabbed the man's wallet as she rabbited. So I had to chase her down to get it. That wallet was rightfully mine after I kilt the guy. She put up a fight; hit me with one of her spiked heels. You oughta see the bruise on my chest. So I hit her back with a brick. You'll find her over there where the trailer park used to be."

Dunk looked over the top of his eyeglasses as if studying a bug. "If you stole the man's wallet, why were you hitting me up for ten dollars? You oughta been buying me drinks instead."

121

Raf lowered his eyes, embarrassed by the failure of his criminal endeavor. "The damn wallet was empty. Guy didn't have a cent on him. He was gonna stiff Glenda for that blowjob, so he deserved everything he got."

Four Fingers wagged his head at Raf's convoluted logic. But, in his experience, criminals were not the smartest people on earth. "Another dead giveaway – no pun. You were looking for a light for a Marlboro. And there's an open pack in the Hummer with one cig missing. You didn't just steal his wallet, you stole a cigarette too."

"Hell, he wasn't gonna smoke it now, was he?"

"One other thing I'm curious about. Why did you tell us about the dead man in the first place? If you'd simply walked away and kept your mouth shut, you might never have been caught."

"Simple. The wallet was empty an' I needed some money. You paid me twenty dollars to show him to you."

"That twenty dollars is going to cost you twenty years – or worse."

"Worse? You mean Old Sparky? No jury in this town's gonna give me a death sentence. I've got too many relatives here. Right, Dunk?"

Raf's cousin shook his head, a grim look on his face as if he'd just sucked on a lime. "Not sure even the Bubba network can save you this time."

Four Fingers pulled his battered Nokia from his pocket. "Hold on while I call Johnny Leigh," he said, dialing the number with his left hand. That missing index finger on his right paw made using a cellphone tricky.

"Sure, take your time. I'm in no hurry to go to Raiford." That's Florida's notorious state prison where Old Sparky resides, although lethal injection is the most common form of execution at FSP these days.

"Raf, you done acted the fool one too many times," said Dunk, starting to sober up. "What am I gonna tell your sainted mama?"

"That she shoulda give me a trust fund like you got. Otherwise, I wouldn't have killed two people over an empty wallet."

"That's your only regret?" asked Dunk. "An empty wallet?"

"No, one other thing."

"What's that?"

"Too bad about Glenda," said Dunk's cousin. "I always had a thing for that gal."

14

Four Fingers and the Minister's Daughter

Wharton "Four Fingers" Dalessandro was not a particularly religious man, but he sometimes had dinner with Rev. Ricky Kagle and his wife Eileen. After all, he was sleeping with their daughter.

Monica Kagle was public information officer for the Key West Police Department, a former reporter with the *Citizen* who had "gone over to the Dark Side," as the paper's editor described anyone who took a higher paying job.

Monica was twice divorced and willing to settle for a Friends With Benefits relationship before going through the nuptials process again. And Four Fingers made a good friend. A lifelong bachelor, he wasn't looking for a serious relationship that might lead to the altar.

Her relationship with Wharton Dalessandro was well known to everybody on the island. There were a limited number of available bed partners of this eight-square-mile rock and after a few round robins you were pretty much up-to-date on who was fucking whom.

Police Chief Johnny Leigh seemed to approve, although he never brought the subject up, his PIO bonking a former NYPD homicide detective who had moved to Key

West about seventeen years ago to paint houses instead of solving crimes. Johnny himself lived with Pete Garoffoli, owner and head chef of Fancy Feast, an upscale pasta restaurant just off Duval. Johnny was mostly Cuban, while Pete was an Eye-talian from New Jersey. Rainbow colors and all that.

Pete Garoffoli didn't see any problem that his trattoria had the same name as a brand of cat food – and neither did the tourists who flocked there night after night. Zagat's rated it 4 stars.

Monica Kagle was a pretty brunette who reminded you of that movie star Angelina Jolie. Those pouty lips were spot-on identical. However, Four Fingers Dalessandro looked nothing like Brad Pitt. If you were casting a movie version of his life, Clive Owen would likely be the star. But with a New York accent.

Four Finger was surprised when he got a message that Rev. Ricky wanted to see him. Other than those polite monthly dinners, the two men rarely encountered each other. Pretending the relationship between the housepainter and the minister's daughter was something other than carnal.

He found Rev. Ricky at the High Seas Methodist Church, that modernistic structure with a sharp spire on the north end of Flagler. He was at the desk in his tiny office working on next Sunday's sermon, a plea for tolerance and increased tithing.

"Rev. Ricky, you wanted to see me?"

The minister raised his shock of white hair. He always reminded Four Fingers of what St. Peter might look like, the gatekeeper who would likely turn him away at the

Pearly Gates. "Oh, thanks for coming. I wanted your advice. A private matter."

Four Fingers wasn't used to playing confessional for a minister. "This doesn't have anything to do with me and Monica? I can explain last Saturday night."

"Oh, I heard about you decking her second ex-husband at the Red Macaw. He deserved it, no doubt. Chimp Lawry was always a troublemaker. He's had run-ins with practically everybody in town. That's why my daughter took back her birth name after the divorce."

"If this isn't about Monica – or Chimp – what could it be?"

"A rather delicate matter. I think a fellow minister here in Key West may have embezzled a rather large sum of money."

Four Fingers looked puzzled. "Another minister?"

"Rev. Benjamin Willingham, pastor of the Fisher of Men Church."

"I've met him. He's tight friends with Mayor Kale and Judge Barbareau. Doesn't seem like the type of man who'd be embezzling money."

Rev. Ricky looked pained to continue. "Then where's the money? Twenty thousand dollars is missing from the God's Help Foundation and Ben's the treasurer."

God's Help was a local charity that was jointly funded by several Key West churches. Its purpose was to provide assistance to homeless families. In this age of foreclosures, God's Help had been particularly active in the island community.

"What does Rev. Benjamin have to say?"

"Ben calls it an accounting error. Claims the twenty thousand was never there in the first place."

Four Fingers thought on it a moment. Legally, he should notify Police Chief Johnny Leigh of a possible crime. But reputations were at stake here. "Got an idea," he said. "Could I use your phone?"

"Help yourself." Rev. Ricky pushed the boxy black handset across the desk toward him. The telephone looked like something out of a 1940s movie.

He dialed a number from memory. "Mayor Kale please," he spoke into the phone. "Tell him it's Wharton Dalessandro." After a moment, he continued, "Hi Henry, got a question. Kinda personal. Did Rev. Benjamin lose any big money recently at your weekly poker games?"

He listened.

"Henry, it's pretty important. Hate to say it, but you owe me one." After a minute he hung up.

"What did you learn?" asked Rev. Ricky.

"Let's go over to the Fisher of Men Church," he said, evading the minister's question.

Rev. Ricky's old oil-guzzling Oldsmobile made it over to Palm Avenue amid chugs, burbs, and backfires. Smoke roiling from its tailpipe would have made you think the car was on fire. Four Fingers expected them to be pulled over by a cop as they drove across the island.

Fisher of Men was more traditional when compared to the modernistic High Seas Methodist Church. A brick building with a steeple, it displayed a sign saying "Follow me, and I will make you fishers of men. – Matthew 4:19." Rev. Benjamin Willingham's sleek new BMW was parked to the side.

They found Rev. Benjamin laying out hymnals in the pews for that night's service. He was a big man with a bullet-shaped head, hairless on top, gray below. His shoulders were wide than a linebackers. Despite his Anglo-Saxon name, his olive-skin was clearly Hispanic in origin. His mother was from Havana, one of the Mariel boat people. He had been a minister in Key West for close to twenty years, after receiving his divinity training at Bob Jones University.

"Hi there, Rev. Ricky. Four Fingers," he greeted them. "I'm expecting a big crowd tonight. They always turn out for the potluck dinner afterwards."

"Way to a man's heart is through his stomach," Rev. Ricky Kagle repeated the old saw. His church socials drew large numbers too.

"Got a private matter to discuss," Four Fingers cut through the pleasantries. "Here okay?"

"Certainly, what has your bowels in an uproar?"

"The missing twenty grand."

Rev. Benjamin spread his hands as if he were Jesus calming the seas. "There is no twenty thousand dollars," he replied. "I tried to explain to Ricky that it was just an accounting error."

Four Fingers shrugged. "Somebody was counting. You paid twenty thousand dollars to Daniel Wallowicz as a poker debt just two weeks ago."

"How did you – ? Oh, that's right, Henry Kale owes you a few favors, getting his daughter off on that murder charge."

"Oh, she murdered the guy all right. Just that there were extenuating circumstances."

129

"Exactly. Like in my case too."

"Isn't Avarice one of the Seven Deadly sins?" commented Four Fingers.

"Maybe to a Catholic. Fisher of Men is a fundamentalist Protestant church."

"Nice car outside."

"Yes, the church provides for me well."

"Sell it. You've got a week."

Rev. Benjamin Willingham looked stricken. "Sell my car?"

"You got it, Reverend. Sell that fancy hunk of iron and repay the money to God's Help. You'll resign as treasurer, pleading pressing church duties. You can keep on ministering to your flock here at Fisher of Men. Or is *flock* the right word for a fishery?"

"You can't make me do that." He looked desperately from Four Fingers to Rev. Ricky and back again.

"Sure I can. You don't do exactly that and I'll put a bug in my friend Johnny Leigh's ear."

"And if I do as you say?"

"Then the matter's settled. I go back to painting houses. You and Rev. Rick keep on saving souls."

As they walked toward Rev. Ricky's dilapidated Oldsmobile, he turned to Four Fingers and said, "You may have saved a soul yourself today."

"Thanks."

"But tell my daughter to phone when she's going to sleep over at your place so we won't worry."

"Yessir," Wharton "Four Fingers" Dalessandro said respectfully. "I'll do that."

↗ ↗ ↗

Thank you for reading.
Please review this book. Reviews help others find me and inspires me to keep writing!

If you would like to be put on our email list to receive updates on new releases, contests, and promotions, please go to AbsolutelyAmazingEbooks.com and sign up.

Bonus

By going to the Absolutely Amazing eBooks website (AbsolutelyAmazingEbooks.com) and entering this password in to the Bonus Reward Section, you can read a totally new Four Fingers Dalessandro mystery – online for **free!**

AA1005

About the Author

Shirrel Rhoades is a writer, critic, filmmaker, former college professor, art collector, and publishing consultant. These days, he calls Key West home. He and his wife share their historic classic temple revival style house in Old Town with a number of dogs and cats and even a pretty TV anchorwoman. But that's another story.

ABSOLUTELY AMAZING eBOOKS

AbsolutelyAmazingEbooks.com
or AA-eBooks.com

Made in United States
Orlando, FL
02 November 2022

24156806R00078